THE WILDEST HUNT

Jo Zebedee

D0784420

Inspired Quill

Published by Inspired Quill: November 2021

First Edition

This is a work of fiction. Names, characters and incidents are the product of the author's imagination. Any resemblance to actual events or persons, living or dead, is entirely coincidental. The publisher has no control over, and is not responsible for, any third-party websites or their contents.

The Wildest Hunt © 2021 by Jo Zebedee

Contact the author through their website: https://jozebedee.com/

LOTTERY FUNDED

Chief Editor: Sara-Jayne Slack
Proofreader: Fiona Lorne
Cover Design: Designs EE
Additional thanks to: Brigid Kapuvari

Typeset in Minion Pro

All Rights Reserved.

No part of this publication may be reproduced or transmitted in any form by any means electronic, mechanical, photocopying, recording or otherwise, without the prior permission of the copyright owner.

Paperback ISBN: 978-1-913117-11-5
eBook ISBN: 978-1-913117-12-2
Print Edition

Printed in the United Kingdom
1 2 3 4 5 6 7 8 9 10

Inspired Quill Publishing, UK
Business Reg. No. 7592847
https://www.inspired-quill.com

Praise for Jo Zebedee

"If there's a line between fantasy and madness, then Jo Zebedee's characters are dragged kicking and screaming across it. A dark fable about belonging that is rooted as deeply in Northern Ireland as it is in the fantasy genre, with shades of Graham Joyce thrown in for good measure."

– Stephen Poore,
Longlist Gemmell Award

"Waters and the Wild had me in suspense from the first page to the last. There are terrible dangers for Amy in both possibilities. Ancient legends meet the modern world in a powerful tale of haunting ambiguities."

– Teresa Edgerton,
author of the *Green Lion* Trilogy

"You need it. So read it."

– Peadar O'Guilin,
author of *The Call*

"Writes characters so close you could touch them."

– *Dan Jones,*
author of *Man O'War*

"A bright and fresh new voice in the genre, brimming with imagination, subtle world building and engaging characters."

– *Francis (Julia) King,*
author of *Fade to Black*

"From first word to last, a pleasure to read."

– J L Dobias,
author of *The Crippled Mode* series

For Chris, Becky and Holly.

traders already beginning to pack their cars.

"Okay," he said at last. "I like Castlewellan. Good for fishing, the lake."

Amelia wrapped the picture with bubble wrap, letting him talk on. He took it from her and she lifted her sketch book as he turned and walked away. She'd finish her sketch of the harbour before packing up. She perched on a bollard and focused on a cluster of boats. Their thin masts reached up in graceful lines, clinking and jangling in the slight breeze, as if singing. Later, when she translated the sketch into a finished picture, she'd pick the fine details out in gold acrylic but, for now, she wanted to capture the feel more than the details.

This was the part she loved. Starting a picture without knowing how it would turn out. It was like stepping into an adventure, a new vision that only emerged when she created it, part of the place and part of her. Her hands sped over the paper, the lines becoming thicker and stronger, darkening as she sketched. It wasn't going to be one of her prettier paintings, but something more naturalist; an Emily Brontë-like rendition of the harbour.

She started to outline the quayside, including a woman who had emerged from one of the boats. Her long dress swept the quay, no doubt picking up every bit of dirt and seagull mess there was. With that and the dark shawl draped over her head, she could have belonged in a picture painted 200 years ago. Amelia's fingers slowed. The lady's dark clothes, combined with the emerging shadowed picture, made her uneasy. The captured line of quayside ended halfway as she put down her pencil. She couldn't feel the picture anymore, couldn't see what it might become when she was finished. Her breathing came too quickly, feather-light. She tried to focus on slowing the breaths, but it made no difference; it still felt like she couldn't force air past her chest.

She stood, setting the notebook beside her car. The market was deserted now – while she had concentrated on her sketching, the other traders had packed up and left. Alone, the carpark felt exposed. Even the wind seemed to have picked up, catching and lifting her hair, as if fingers were running through it.

Quickly, with jerky fingers, she stacked what was left of her prints into their box, setting it into the boot of her car. She'd finish the sketch from memory. She slammed the boot closed.

A sound behind her made her turn, heart beating too hard, but there was no one on the quayside except the lady at the other side of the harbour. Her eyes fixed on Amelia's, dark under the shadow of her scarf. Her dress soaked up the pool of water beneath her feet, briny and dirty with oil, but she didn't seem to notice.

Amelia's panic built further. It was ridiculous; an eccentrically-dressed old lady wasn't anything to be scared of. Even so, she had to get away from this place. She backed up to the driver's door.

Her hand brushed the handle just as the lady began to wail. Amelia clapped her hands over her ears, but the woman kept screeching; long screams that rose and fell and didn't stop. Nothing appeared to be wrong with her: no visible marks, or injuries. No-one else close by to aggravate her. Just the screams.

A hand grabbed Amelia's elbow from behind. She

female medic helped her to her feet. She looked about twenty, too young to have such a responsible job, surely. Sam had stopped trying to speak, hadn't moved, was still and white-faced. Amelia wanted to ask if he'd be okay but was too worried what the answer would be.

The crew checked him over, fitting a mask to his face and swiftly, gently, injecting him. They gently moved him onto a stretcher and lifted him into the ambulance.

She had to know. She touched the arm of the paramedic who had moved her.

"Is he....?" *What to ask? Is he dead? Or would he make it? What platitude was the right one?*

The paramedic might be young but she was calm. "He's very poorly but we'll do what we can." She rubbed Amelia's shoulders. "Is there someone you can call? It's a shock, when these things happen."

Amelia shook her head. She couldn't bring Joe all this way – and, anyway, she had the car. The ambulance pulled out, through the crowd. No sirens sounded. The air was strangely silent: it took a moment for Amelia to realise that even the screams from the lady at the harbour had stopped.

"Do you want a cup of tea?" asked Elizabeth. "I can easily make some."

Amelia shook her head. "I was just here for the market." She had to get home to Joe, he'd steady her. She turned to go, but stopped, the man's words nagging at her. "What did he mean, The Grey Lady?"

"It's just an old superstition," said Elizabeth. "You know how these things are."

She didn't really, but she knew small towns. If this lady

had decided she wasn't going to tell, then she wouldn't. Even so, Amelia couldn't leave it alone. The memory of the screeching woman on the quay was still too raw.

"I saw someone," she said. "On the quay. She was dressed in old clothes, and making a desperate noise."

Elizabeth's mouth had tightened into a thin line. "Perhaps you should head home."

There was no point in arguing. The conversation was clearly over. Amelia took a last look at the empty harbour, the boats bobbing gently. No old woman. No shrieks.

Slowly, Amelia made her way back to her car, slid into the driver's seat and carefully rolled out of the car park, all under Elizabeth's watchful gaze. She was halfway to Newry before she remembered the sketchbook she'd dropped.

CHAPTER TWO
Templeton House

THE PHONE RANG, loud in the high-ceilinged hall. Jean hurried across the vast hallway, trying to outrace the answer machine. She grabbed the handset, just as it clicked to transfer, and stabbed the button.

"Templeton House, Mrs Sweeney speaking."

She still loved how that sounded. Templeton House, where she never dreamed of living in as a child. And Mrs Sweeney, not Jean, which told people she had been the one to fight hard enough, and long enough, to capture Robert, heir to his father's fortune.

A man at the other end of the line cleared his throat. "Paddy from Castlewellan here, Mrs Sweeney." He had a broad country accent, so thick Jean struggled to understand him.

"Yes?" she said. Perhaps he'd offer to do some work on the house, like the fellows who turned up every summer, offering to do the driveway. Travelers, quite clearly, not the sort of workmen Robert would tolerate.

"You asked me to be on the look out," said Paddy.

"For books and objects."

Now she remembered the man. Based in a rotting barn that he claimed was an antiques shop. It had been filthy, she recalled. Not a place she would normally visit.

"I've found something," he said.

Her eyelid twitched, but she held herself in check. She'd had other such calls before. All, once investigated, had proved useless: false mediums using crystal balls made of lumps of glass, or wise women who turned out not to have second-sight but a nosiness that kept them in secrets for years.

"Go on," she said.

"There was a death in Newcastle at the weekend," said Paddy-from-Castlewellan. "Sam from one of the local families said the Grey Lady turned up."

He didn't give any more details, so Jean had to ask: "The who turned up?"

"The Grey Lady. She's a banshee."

Of course she was. Probably the man's sister, done up in a shawl and wailing in the hope of getting paid. Even if it had been plausible, a banshee wasn't what she needed: a banshee knew what was to come, not what had been. Her free hand twitched, ready to end the call.

"One of the people who helped was an artist."

"Yes?" By goodness, he was long-winded.

"Well, she saw the banshee. Better than that – she drew it." He paused. "Or, at least, we think that's what she drew. She certainly talked about seeing it. And the picture looks like any I've ever seen of the banshee."

So what? The words were on the tip of Jean's tongue, when his meaning sank in. She had to grab the wall to steady herself. "Did anyone else see this... Grey Lady?" Her heart drummed uncomfortably in her chest. She was offering a decent reward; this man could be scamming her. But she knew that he wasn't, that this was the real thing, by the shiver that ran down her spine.

"Only Sam. But my sister Elizabeth works in the bar. She was there, and she heard the artist ask about the Grey Lady. She knows I'm on the look out for this kind of thing. When the artist woman left and she saw the picture, she grabbed it for me. I have it now."

"You stole it?" Not that she cared. She'd done worse things over the years.

"Naw." He sounded a little hurt. "She left it behind. The Grey Lady is in it, I swear she is. The artist *definitely* saw the banshee." Another pause. She could practically hear the cogs turning in the man's head. "Do I get my cut, Mrs Sweeney? I know it was objects I was to keep an eye out for, from house sales and the like, but this might still be useful? I have the picture, and the artist's number and address. Our Jim works at the council, where they hired out the stalls for the fair, and he slipped it to me. And her website – she has other pictures on it."

Jean made sure to hide that she was secretly impressed. "Indeed you should get your cut." A contact was a contact, and he'd been a useful one. "Paddy, wasn't it? Let me give you my email." She read it out and had him read it back. "Please send me a copy of the picture. Plus the bank account I should send remittance to. Now, what is the website, please?"

Carefully she typed it into her smartphone. Pictures appeared, a good number of them, all landscapes. Few stood out and none screamed of any psychic ability. She scrolled to the second page and stopped. One picture was darker than its companions, taking her attention in a way the others had not. She zoomed in, using her fingers to make the picture as detailed as possible. It was a seascape, captured on a wild day when the water seemed to rake to land, so strong were the brush strokes. She could nearly taste the tang of brine and the sudden chill of a squall.

A building loomed in the picture's background, its single tower stretching like a finger against a darkened sky. Familiar from tourist pictures of the North Coast: Ballygally Castle, the hotel with the supposed ghost. Leaning in, she was able to make out the smallest smudge of white at the top window, from the supposed ghost-room in the castle's turret. Looked at from a certain angle it appeared to be a face, milky-white and barely there.

The ping of an incoming email drew her attention away. Quickly, she opened the attachment. The drawing of the harbour was rough, obviously a working sketch, but that it had been drawn by the same artist was undeniable in its strong resemblance to the structure and feel of the Ballygally picture. Jean found herself pulling her sleeves over her wrists to keep a sudden chill at bay.

The harbour in the painting felt both bleak and oddly beautiful. But that wasn't what took Jean's breath away. She ran her finger along the screen, stopping at the centre of the drawing. There, just as Paddy had promised, hidden amongst the boats, stood the undeniable figure of an old woman. This artist *was* the real thing. Finally, she might get the answer she'd waited forty years for.

CHAPTER THREE

A Commission

"YOU'RE SURE THIS Sweeney woman was serious?" Joe, in the driver's seat, glanced over at Amelia. "She wants to pay you fifteen grand to paint a picture of some house?"

"So she says." And it wasn't like they were in the position to turn the money down, even if the prospect of another chocolate-box painting depressed her. For fifteen grand, she'd paint whatever the lady wanted, wherever and however she wanted it. She'd even do it in the nude, if asked. "Let's see what she says, though."

"I'm telling you now, there's bound to be a catch," said Joe. "It's too good to be true."

"I think you're right." Although she couldn't think of what kind of catch there might be. A painting was a painting. Unless there was something illegal involved.

"Well, she definitely has money, living round here," said Joe. "Look at these houses. It's like Escape to the Country, live."

She didn't want to guess at the sort of prices these

houses must fetch. Deep into rural privacy, but only ten minutes from the sea and less than an hour from the city. Maybe this Jean Sweeney just didn't know the value of that much cash. Fifteen grand was probably clothes money to her.

They turned off an already-narrow road onto a country lane, bumping along for a mile or so before passing through a narrow gateway flanked by stone stallions – of course, there would have to be stone animals – and into a wide sweep of driveway surrounding a central lawn. An elegant three-storey house stood just ahead. No wonder they hadn't been able to find it without asking directions in the village they'd passed through three times.

"My God," said Joe. "That's a serious pile."

"That's not all." Amelia pointed to their right, along a short woodland path. In a field at the bottom, two horses grazed: they might even be thoroughbreds by the look of their long necks and nervous head-tosses as the car passed. Beyond that, a paddock glinted dully in the sun, low jumps laid out, and several barns stood open. "I think they might have a stud-farm."

"Well, that answers one question," said Joe. "She has the money."

"She *did* sound posh."

"Posh? This is bloody landed gentry."

They parked in the shadow of the house and began to make their way to the porch. Amelia craned her head back and tried to count windows but felt too much like a gawking tourist and stopped.

The house was as broad as it was tall. Worry wormed

you can get the staff in to look it over if you need to."

The staff. Robert made it sound so grand, not a half-hearted agreement with two locals to keep an eye on things at the house. They'd have been round today, leaving the tree in and airing the house so that the young couple would not realise it hadn't been used since the end of the summer and the tourist season. She didn't want them to have any idea that it had been important – essential – for them to be there in the darkest days around the Solstice.

"I don't even know why you keep it." His eyes flickered towards Belle's picture and away. "It's not as if it makes any difference to her."

She ignored his comment. Robert was unpleasant about anything to do with Donegal, let alone Donegal in the winter. If he knew about the artist, the conversation would descend into the cold fury she hated from him.

He frowned. "You seem very unsettled, Jean."

She realised, too late, that she had been nibbling the edge of her nails, a nervous response she'd never been able to train herself out of. Hurriedly, she brought her hands down and clasped them together in her lap.

"You know me." She gave a half-laugh. "I just worry about things. That's all. Nothing else."

He didn't give any indication of whether he knew she was lying about something, damn him, and he probably did. He was preternatural, Robert. Even as a child, he'd been able to work out what people were thinking and how it made them tick. He'd led something of a campaign of terror against those who crossed him at school, choosing the thing they were most ashamed of and ensuring those they most respected found out. With age, he'd become less cruel – by and large – but no less effective. If he found out the truth of what she had done, sending the artist to Glenveagh, his revenge would be efficient and effective, perhaps a whisper to the town gossip-machine about the weight she was struggling to shift, or a sudden decision to sell a horse she'd become attached to.

THE SILENCE BETWEEN them stretched, not companionable. Their silences never were. The white lights on the Christmas tree in the corner blinked on and off, on and off, marking time. She wished she'd bought a warmer colour. At last, she could bear the silence no longer, although Robert appeared unperturbed.

"Oh well, you know Donegal," she said, forcing a lightness. "They're used to rough weather. The cottage will stay standing."

A muscle twitched in Robert's cheek and she regretted returning to the subject. He'd – *they'd* – lost Belle during a terrible winter there. So many people had died that season – one bright spark, near Limavady, had driven his jeep onto a frozen pond and had been dragged through the cracked ice, the horror pictures splashed all over the newspapers at the time; at least, until the news broke about Belle. The ten-year-old daughter of Campbell Sweeney, lawyer and landowner, found dead in a freezing outdoor pool during a family holiday would have knocked any story off the front page: the lack of suspects and the bleak landscape of Glenveagh had the press in a frenzy. That the person to find her body had been her stunned brother, Robert, heir to the Sweeney fortune, had only fueled more

CHAPTER SIX

Night Visitors

AMELIA WOKE WITH the covers pulled over her head and her butt burrowed against the only marginally warmer Joe. The thick duvet, covered by two blankets taken from the upstairs' bedrooms, had made little impact on the cold but, in the end, the bed had been preferable to the sofa.

She shook her head, groggy, reviving the dull throbbing that had wakened her in the night. Since then, her sleep had been chased by dreams, half-vanished now, leaving only a memory of hunting horns and the heavy sound of hooves. She'd thought the noises might be coming from the small garden around the house but, of course, that was ridiculous. Nothing would have been hunting on such a wild night.

Cautiously, knowing her hope was misplaced, Amelia reached across the narrow gap to the radiator, but its frigid metal spoke of many idle hours. She drew her hand back under the covers to warm up, but the air that edged around her was chill and sharp. Nothing for it: she had to get moving.

Grimacing, she ducked out from under the duvet, grabbing her fleece from a chair and a pair of thick socks from her open hold-all. She crossed the narrow hall to the living room, hoping it would be warmer but without any slack over the coals to keep the fire lit, it had died overnight.

Amelia pulled her fleece on and drew back the curtains. In spite of the cold, she let out a gasp. The sky was deceptively blue and the snow-covered garden could have been used in any White-Christmas promo shot. In the distance, darker clouds wreathed the mountains, as ominous as the previous night's weather forecast.

"Merry Christmas," she murmured to herself, but it didn't feel like Christmas Day with its usual bustle and chaos and frantic dashing from present opening, to her parents' house, and on to Joe's dysfunctional mother's for dinner. She touched the ring on her finger, tracing the sharp cut of the single diamond, and that made the sense of a special – different – Christmas day more real.

A low groan told her Joe had reached consciousness. A moment later he appeared in the doorway. Even he, who normally slept with no top, impervious to the cold, had pulled on a sweater. His bare legs were goosebumped and thin, as if his muscles had shrunk back from the frigid air.

"Bloody hell," he said. "It's Baltic."

She knelt by the fire and nudged it with the iron poker, hoping for some kind of reward, but the peat-shaped mounds fell into brown dust, lifeless and useless.

"What should we do?" she asked.

He squinted out the window. "It must have snowed

half the night."

"It's to keep up," she said. "The clouds over the mountains look ominous."

"I remember." His voice had turned grim, and that wasn't like Joe who was one of life's copers. It worried her that he was worried. "If we stay, we run the risk of getting stranded if the snow does close in again. I say we take the break in the weather, and go."

"I agree." Not just because of the prospect of being snowed in but because of her creeping dreams of the night before, the nagging sense that something really could be outside the cottage, stalking them. She understood how silly that sounded, but… she'd always had her odd feelings. The day at the harbour, with the Grey Lady and the dead man. At Ballygally with the ghost. As a child, in the tomb grave, when the walls had switched and changed and the dead had risen around her. She knew a dream was just a dream, but she also knew it might not be.

"I'll get our stuff together," she said.

"I'll try the car."

She went back to the bedroom, steeling herself, and pulled off her pyjamas. Joe followed and it was testament to the cold that he didn't pay any attention to her, but instead stripped, swearing, before pulling on his jeans. She put a pair of thick tights under hers and added two pairs of socks. It made it hard to pull on her jeans but she persevered. She layered her top half, too: a t-shirt under a long-sleeve top, a thin fleece and, finally, a sweater. She dug out her walking boots, comforted by their familiar heaviness.

Feeling like an astronaut, ungainly and heavy, she

made her way to the hallway. She tugged open the front door, which gave with a groan.

Whiteness stretched. It was beautiful, to be somewhere so remote, so alone, and have this at their doorstep. It might not have been the Christmas they'd planned, but she'd never forget this moment, suspended in a world that felt cut off from anyone or anywhere.

"One giant step for womankind." She stepped out. "One… bugger!" She stumbled off the end of the step. Her yell carried in the still air, startling a robin as if she had invaded its world. She tried to dig her heels in, to catch herself, but tumbled down the hill, arms flailing for purchase.

She came to a halt at the end of the driveway, only stopping herself from hurtling into the lane by grabbing the gate post, wrenching her arm in the process. She managed to get her other hand on the gate and stood balanced, precariously and ungainly, between the post and gate. No more pain hit; it seemed the snow had protected her, but her heart still raced. Another foot or two, and she wouldn't have been able to stop. The hill was steep enough that she could have been really hurt.

She took a moment to gather herself together. Joe knew her too well – if he saw her right now he'd know that she'd frightened herself, and they were both worried enough already.

A disturbed patch of snow, just beyond the gateway, caught her eye. The marks didn't look like foxes. They were too big. A finger of warning went down her spine, a tickle of something she couldn't describe any more than she could ignore it. She leaned in closer, using the gate for support to stop her hurtling down the slope. The marks looked like hoof-prints, but they'd merged together and it was difficult to make out individual tracks. It could have been one animal or ten. Big, by the look of it. The dream-memory of drumming hooves, the sureness something was in the garden came back, sharply dangerous. She drew back.

"Joe!" she called. To hell with him knowing that she was rattled. "Come and see this."

He came quickly, on too-high alert. His fleece made him look twice his normal size.

"Hey, Mrs Stay-Puff. Meet the Michelin Man. Classy," he said. "Jesus, this is deep." He crouched and put his gloved hand against the snow, pushing down so that his whole fist was swallowed. "Another dump and we *will* be snowed in."

"Joe…?" she said.

"What?"

"There was something here last night." She tapped the edge of the broken hoof prints with her toecap, still not sure why she didn't want to go nearer. "Any idea what it might have been?"

"Deer," said Joe. He sounded sure. "They're all over the mountains."

He could be right, but still the cold warning stayed with her. The tracks were big, even for a large roe deer. A shadow fell, bringing a sudden cold, and she looked up. The last patch of blue had clouded over, turning the sky to slate-grey.

"I think we should get underway," said Joe. "What do you reckon about breakfast on the run?"

"Sounds good." She went back to the house, his hand on her butt 'to help her up the hill' and that, at least, made her laugh. Ever the opportunist, Joe. He disappeared around the back of the house but reappeared a moment later, carrying a shovel, and began to work around the car, shifting the snow from behind its wheels. He worked quickly, methodically. Once, he looked over his shoulder, frowning at the tracks and she knew that he, too, didn't think they belonged to deer.

She began to repack the few bags they'd bothered to empty. The house was cold and dead-feeling, and the unlit Christmas tree looked sorry for itself, not nearly cheery as it had been. From outside, the steady crunch-crunch of Joe's shovel carried. In the kitchen she made up a snatch-pack of chocolate and crisps. She broke a croissant as she worked, glad of something stodgy and comforting.

"Times like this a tractor would be good," said Joe, startling her. He, too, took a croissant, devouring it in two bites. "How are we doing? Ready?"

"Pretty much." She emptied the contents of the fridge into a bag: a chicken, ready-made roasties and veg, milk, a couple of bottles of wine and Joe's remaining beer. The more portable items; the crisps, some oat bars, and chocolate, she put into the rucksack.

"Ready!" She followed Joe to the car, food bag over her shoulder. The snow fell with intent. Joe chucked their rucksack into the boot. "Let's get on the road."

Amelia locked the cottage's door and posted the key. She clumped over to the passenger side and put some of the chocolate supplies in the well of her seat. Already the cleared windscreen had filled with fresh snow. Worry gnawed at her, that they'd missed their chance to go. No, more than that: it felt like something didn't want them to leave.

"Right," Joe said, his breath white. "Here goes nothing."

He threw the shovel into the boot of the car, muttering that he could be sued for it, and turned the key. The car gave a cough, but died. Amelia's hands tightened into fists. *Work. Come on, work.* Joe tried again, but the car still didn't turn over. She glanced sharply at him but his face was impossible to read. Joe tried again and this time the car tried to catch, whining and choking and then giving up.

"Just cold," he said, but didn't meet her eyes. He gave the key another sharp twist, giving the car time to catch until, at last, it roared to life. Joe revved the engine and grinned. "See? That was close."

The car idled as the engine warmed, but it missed more than one beat. The hill to the lane looked ominous, as if the car could tip down it, and the lane itself was steeper again. Fresh snow had started to fill in the animal's tracks. Could her and Joe's presence be erased just as easily? She wished she hadn't thought that, and tried to reassure herself that whoever had put up the Christmas tree must know someone was staying at the cottage. They weren't alone out in these mountains, others *did* live in the area. But it didn't feel like it.

Joe let the handbrake off and the car started down the hill. He held his foot lightly on the brake, keeping the speed under control. "There's not much grip."

She could feel the car threatening to fishtail. Joe held it

steady as they descended, the gear high enough to give some control. They crawled to the lane, turning a careful right, but it wasn't any better. Mountains loomed on both sides, white and treacherous.

Joe hunched forwards, his eyes on the road. Amelia, selfishly, was glad he was driving. The blue sky was already a thing of the past, eaten up by this monster of a storm. A gust of wind buffeted them, whistling around the windows, as if trying to get in. The windscreen wipers made little impact and Joe switched the full-beams on. They reflected yellow in the snow, highlighting the main mountain road just ahead. It was wider, and straighter, but the conditions little better.

"Should be off the choke soon," Joe said, more worried than she liked. She glanced sharply at him but he kept his eyes on the road. "Knew I should have booked a service."

Joe never liked to admit the car needed more than his attention. Amelia ran her fingers along the door's handrest, as if comforting the car and willing it to keep going. It skidded, the back end swerving onto the wrong side of the road. Joe swore; Amelia's stomach hit the roof of her mouth.

"Maybe we should go back," she said. "We have food. We could wait out the storm." Sure, it had been cold. But they could light the fire and stay in the living room. Briefly, she wondered if it was possible to cook a chicken on an open fire. She'd likely food poison them and top off the weekend.

"How?" said Joe.

"We could park on the road and walk back up."

"That's only half the problem. We've no key."

Damn. She shouldn't have posted it. The snow was horizontal now, battering her side of the car. Panic threatened, a sick knowledge they were on their own, reliant on a car that could break down at any moment, but she bit it down. Panic would get her nowhere.

"Don't worry," Joe said, but his voice was tight and cautious. "In another ten miles or so we'll hit the main road."

Ten miles? In this? But she didn't say it. Silence fell between them. The car's beat settled down, and she started to hope everything would be okay.

A light came up on the dashboard and flashed insistently.

"Joe…." she said.

"I know. She's overheating." Joe dropped down a gear. "Grip's awful."

"Will we be all right?"

"Hope so."

"We have breakdown cover. That's something."

"Think again." Joe risked a quick glance at her. "We have breakdown cover in the North. Which is miles from where we are."

Hell, he was right – the all-Ireland option had been too expensive. Even if the break-down truck could have reached them on this mountain. There was nothing for it but to go on. The windscreen wipers beat a steady rhythm but the snow was falling too hard and fast, covering the glass in seconds. The car's temperature gauge crept up: she couldn't take her eyes off it.

"We're going to have to pull over," said Joe. "If we don't, we could blow something."

"Here?" Outside was white nothingness.

"Not on the road – too dangerous. I'd be lucky not to end up in a ditch. We're not far from the country park, though."

"So?"

"We'll pull in there and let the engine cool. The facilities are closed, and so is the big house, but the estate itself is always open. Watch for the signs – we could sail right past in this."

She strained her eyes, seeking through the gloom. They passed no other cars. The locals were used to rough weather, half of them had 4 by 4s and a fair few had tractors. Surely some would have ventured out, maybe to visit relatives, or to attend Christmas Day Mass? But it seemed not.

Something appeared on the right, blurring into a tourist sign. "Coming up," she said.

Joe nodded. The road into the estate appeared. He turned in, keeping the car under tight control. Trees loomed on either side, their branches heavy with snow, but at least the road was straight.

A hare appeared before them, right in the centre of the road.

"Joe!" she said.

"I know!" He hit the brakes. Amelia was thrown forwards as the brakes locked.

"Hold on!" yelled Joe. The car skidded. Any semblance of control was gone. Branches pinged off the car windows. One scraped the length of the windscreen. The car rutted and bumped, hurtling down a bank and gaining speed. A fallen tree appeared out of the gloom, dead ahead.

"Joe!"

He wrenched the wheel to the side, forearms corded with desperate strength, but the car hit with a bone-shaking thud. The last thing Amelia saw, before things went black, was the hare hopping away, as if its job was done.

CHAPTER SEVEN
Glenveagh

COLD AIR BROUGHT Amelia round, followed by a thumping pain above her right eye. She blinked, clearing the darkness. She didn't know where she was, or what had happened. Something thudded, followed by a slicing noise and more thudding, and it didn't make sense.

A moment later, in startling clarity, the crash came back to her: the skid, the tree, the hare that had caused it hopping away.

Slowly, she felt around, crabbing her hand, not daring to move too much. The seat underneath her was tilted at the wrong angle. With a groan, she turned her head. Their poor car – unloved, unserviced, and now in a mess – lay at a 45-degree angle, her door towards the ground. Snow lay outside, visible through her window and blue in the shadow of the car, and she could see that it had formed a bank only a few inches away. That bank might have saved her, she guessed, by stopping the car rolling. Certainly, the punched-out lung of a deflated airbag told her they'd hit something hard.

Her breath caught. "Joe…?" The driver's seat was empty but its door was open, pushed far enough to hold. She could see only trees and snow beyond. No Joe.

She scrabbled for her seat belt, hands shaking from the biting cold, and managed to unclick it. The car creaked ominously. She had no idea how it was balanced on Joe's side. If she caused it to shift that way, would there be another bank of snow to stop her, or would it just keep on rolling? Cold air flowed around her and she looked from Joe's door, to the snow bank outside. If she made the wrong move, she could be dead.

She studied Joe's seat, raised above her. She couldn't get out her own side. Even if the door opened, the snow would block it and she'd be trapped under the tilted car. But if she could make it to Joe's door, that might work. He'd obviously managed to get out. She took her time, plotting how to get over there. She would only get one chance at it; once shifted, she'd have to get clear of the car. She put one hand on his seat and found it wet and sticky under her palm. She dreaded what that might mean.

Biting down visions of chasms beyond, she carefully – oh, so carefully – climbed onto Joe's seat, thankful for the open central divide. Creaks came from all around. The car's weight moved, threatening to drop at Joe's side. Everything in her screamed to stop but she could see the open door and smell the air beyond that meant freedom and a way out of this mess.

She made it onto Joe's seat. For a heart-stopping moment she thought the car would roll, and prepared herself for a drop, but it settled back, leaving her looking at a tilted world beyond the windscreen. She put her hand down, bracing herself, and craned her head to see out of the driver's door.

"Joe…?" Her voice croaked. No answer came. She swallowed dryness and raised her voice. "Joe!"

Had he wandered off, confused? The stickiness of the seat told her he'd hurt himself and she could think of no other reason why he'd leave her, not even to get help. Surely, he'd have tried to get her out first.

"Amelia!" Joe's shout was quick, and sharp, almost panicked. "Don't move!"

The urgency in his voice stopped her just before she sprang forwards. She stayed where she was, tight against the seat and craned her head, just a little more. It confirmed what she had feared: her only hope was a smooth jump out of the car and onto the snow. It would take a gymnast to carry it off, and that certainly wasn't her. She stayed tight where she was, palms sweating. She hated her own fear.

Joe came into sight, appearing from behind the car. A long gash ran along one side of his face, the blood a dark line, but otherwise he seemed unhurt. "Stay really still."

"What do I do?" She fought to keep her voice steady. "I can't stay here."

"I'm going to shovel snow along the chassis," he said. "It should stabilise the car." He ran a hand through his hair, making it tuft up, and he looked about fifteen, not his mid-twenties. "Jesus. You scared me. You were out cold. When I got out and saw where we were…."

"How did you get out?"

"I jumped."

Which was what she'd been planning to do. She took a

deep breath. "I can do that too."

"No!" His face told her all she needed to know. "You were in the passenger seat when I got out. Extra weight – you were the ballast." His hands were shaking, she noted. "Sit tight, don't move and I'll get back to shovelling."

He disappeared. She tried to crane her head to see where he was and what he was doing but the car shifted and she concentrated on staying very, very still. *Come on, Joe. Get on with it.*

The sound of snow crunching and thudding came in a rhythm. She hoped Joe knew what he was doing. She imagined the car was moving each time he put a shovel-load down, twisting at the front end. The image of it crashing downwards, the imagined fear of long moments of knowledge as she fell, threatened to swamp her.

At the next shovel there the car *did* shift slightly.

"Joe!" she called. "I think you should stop."

He mustn't have heard her, because there was another scrape and a thud. The front of the car loosened. Working at the back, he might not notice.

"Joe!" Still nothing. Another thud. Another jolt. Another moment of heart-stopping knowledge that the car could go at any moment.

Her hands moved without thought, the first taking hold of the door lip, the other hard against the seat behind her. She could see the dip, just below her. Her muscles were cramped from so long in the cold. She'd have one chance.

Another crunch of spade through snow. The long moment before Joe would thud it down, pushing the car once more and she knew it was close to giving and that she was out of time.

With a yell, she pulled herself out of the car with one hand, pushing from behind with the other. She tumbled out, the snow cold and hard against her cheek when she landed. She rolled, aiming for the front of the bank and yelled as she jolted against it. Instinct made her curl into a ball.

Car metal squealed. Snow shifted around her. The bank became less solid.

"Amelia!" Joe's shout rang loud and desperate.

Metal shrieked. Amelia ducked her head further in, contorting her spine. She brought her hands over her head, as if that might help. A juddering, knocking moment of horror came as the car tumbled over her. She waited for pain, for the heaviness of metal on her. She would have screamed, but didn't have the breath, squashed up as she was. Somewhere, she thought Joe might be yelling, but it was lost in the crunch of metal.

The noise carried on, a great, long, thundering. The smell of oil was all around her. She wanted to get up, to run, but didn't move, her teeth gritted in the determination to stay still.

At last, the rumbling stopped. Something touched her back, making her tense.

"Amelia. Can you move?"

Cautiously, she looked to her right. Joe crouched beside her. She peered beyond him, down a short, but increasingly steep, hill. At the bottom lay their car, its front end smashed and twisted. Only the lip of the bank had saved her.

"Can you speak?" asked Joe. "Are you all right? Are

you hurt?"

He didn't want to move her, she realised. She uncurled herself from the ball, wincing at a pain in her knee and the thudding in her head. "I'm okay." She thought so, anyway. "The front end was coming free. I had to jump."

"Jesus." He was pale. "I'm sorry. I thought…" But he didn't say what he thought. His throat rippled as he swallowed. "Hell, we needed stuff from the car. Food. Cold weather gear. My hiking rucksack has all that."

"Then we need to get to the car," she said. She stood. Her legs didn't feel solid. The ground looked too far away. Her right wrist ached and her left knee felt twisted and bruised. She stared down the hill. On a nice day it would have presented no problems but in the snow and ice the slope would be lethal. "Right. What's our best way down?"

"I'll go," said Joe. "You rest."

"No." They were not getting separated again. "Together." She stretched her arms, not showing the pain in her wrist, and gave a little jump. "I'm fine. See?"

Joe stood beside her, looking down at the car. "If we do this, we do it carefully." Taking his own advice, he grabbed the nearest tree and lowered himself down the hill. He reached his free hand to Amelia. "One tree at a time."

That was the only thing for it. One problem at a time. Reach the car. Get supplies. Then get help. Each action was a single step, the whole picture a panic-inducing mountain of fear it would do her no good to think about.

She slid down to where Joe was, waiting as he traversed the next part of the slope, the ground cut up by the car's fall, and took his hand as he helped her down.

One step at a time. *Deal with this part, and then the next, until they were safe, and never dare to think they might not be.*

THE CAR, WHEN they reached it, was a sorry sight. Terminal, by the look of it, and she didn't think about that, either. Without the money from the commission a new one was out of the question.

Joe gave a smile that was more of a grimace. "At least we saved on the service.... The only thing she's good for is scrap."

Amelia crouched at the boot. It was twisted, but not as smashed in as the front end. "I think we should be able to get it open."

"Good. I don't have a crowbar handy." He joined her. "Plus, we really, *really* need the rucksack. And whatever food is portable. I don't know what time it is, but it must be into the afternoon."

"Where's your phone?" she asked. The snow still fell steadily but much less like the storm of earlier. As if, having brought them here, the snow had finished its work. A ridiculous thing to think, it made no sense; except when it made too much sense.

"No charge. Remember, no power last night?"

Joe drained batteries listening to music like no one else could. She fished around in her pocket, wincing as her wrist jarred, and found her own phone but when she brought it out, the display was cracked. She tried the power key, but it remained dead.

"This day just keeps getting better," said Joe. "There goes plan A: find somewhere with reception and call for help."

"And plan B is?"

He ran his hands along the edge of the car boot, no doubt trying to feel for the catch. "Take shelter until the weather eases – there should be some if we find the main estate. The fact that it's Christmas won't stop the hikers. I'd say if the snow holds off there will be someone attempting the hills by tomorrow. There might even be people around today, but we'd be lucky to run into them. Tomorrow, we can stake out the car park."

"We could walk for help," she said. "We're not far from a village, if I'm right."

"We could also walk out and end up lost on the Donegal mountains where there's no shelter and no one is likely to come past. Safer to stay here, I think." He frowned, and wriggled his fingers into a gap between the boot and its hood. "First things first…. You take the right side, and I'll try the left. The catch feels off centre."

She did, and they tried lifting the boot but it didn't give. Joe crouched, trying to stare through the crack. "Try again. Force it a little to the right."

She did. He wriggled his hand further into the crack, until his fingers were inside. Her mouth was dry. If the boot shifted his fingers would be trapped. She concentrated on keeping as much of the weight off him as she could.

"Come on, come on," said Joe, grimacing. At last there was a sharp crack and she was able to wriggle her own fingers under. Between them they forced the boot partially open.

"Yes!" said Joe. He pushed the boot up further. The metal shrieked in protest but it was enough – they could get to the contents.

Amelia grabbed Joe's rucksack. It had been packed for their planned hill-walking, and was the best sight she'd had all day. She tugged it free from the rest of their gear, jumbled around in the crash, and handing it to Joe. He shrugged it on, shifting his shoulders so that it lay comfortably.

"We need to find cover," she said.

"Yep. If we get into the estate, there should be shelter."

If. She couldn't see any sign of the lough that formed the central feature of the estate, which would have allowed them to find their bearings. She stamped her feet, trying to get some heat into them. Self-pity threatened but there was no time for it. People who survived were active. They took the steps needed to make it through, and not one of those steps consisted of merely hoping for the best. She forced a smile, slight though it was. "Well, let's get going, then."

Joe gave a mock-salute. "Yes, ma'am." He started to clamber back up the hill. "The road we were on led towards the main estate. If we follow our crash-line we'll come out where we need to."

She climbed the hill, grateful for each one of her aches and pains: it meant she was alive, not crushed.

Where there was life, there was hope.

CHAPTER EIGHT

Christmas Morning in Paradise

THE TELEVISION NEWS played coverage of the Christmas day chaos at every showing. Power cuts, roads closed, and at least one fatal accident. Some more humorous stories of people eating cold beans for Christmas lunch. Donegal had apparently been half-flattened by conditions that were unprecedented in terms of the speed at which the storm had closed in, leaving people unprepared and the county in shutdown.

Jean picked up the phone handset and hit the redial option to connect to the cottage. The dead tone came again. She tried Amelia's mobile number but it went straight to answerphone. Rationality told her the electricity must be off in the cottage – it went down a couple of times a year, generally – and phone lines felled. But there was still the fire in the living room and, so long as one room was warm, the couple should be safe. Not being able to get a reply didn't mean there was something wrong.

She realised she was chewing an expensively

manicured nail and took it from her mouth, absentmindedly running her thumb along its edge to assess the damage.

She could give the O'Neills, who looked after the cottage, a ring. But what good would that do? She couldn't ask them to drive across the mountains in such atrocious conditions, not at their age, and especially not on Christmas Day.

"Half an hour, Jean!" Robert, still blithely unaware, had flung himself into their own Christmas morning tradition, when half the village would drop over for drinks and nibbles. The other half would be there, too, but they'd be there to assess the Big House's value, running costs and internal state. Last year she'd found three ladies in the drawing room, not-so-surreptitiously confirming her throw had been purchased from Avoca and not Tesco.

Jean set the phone down. Normally by now she'd have checked every room in the house for tidiness – today she'd barely confirmed the dining table was laid and the best china out.

She crossed to the window and stared outside. Not a speck of snow had fallen. In fact, for a winter's day it felt quite warm. Yet only a hundred or so miles away Snowmageddon had apparently arrived. It made no sense.

Christmas lights lined each side of the avenue leading around the lawned area, showing off its symmetry and, in turn, the grandness of the house and garden. Normally that would have pleased her; today it felt hollow.

"Here you go." Robert handed her a traditional Christmas sherry which she took automatically. He had his Christmas jumper on, the one with Rudolph and a line of jingly bells. It made her feel too dressed up in her cocktail dress but she'd never been able to bring herself to dress down at Christmas: her parents had drilled it into her that it was a special day, when the normal rules were suspended.

"Everything's ready," he said, but she didn't reply. He threw her a mutinous look, eyes narrowed. "Don't mention it."

God, Robert could be so needy. All he'd done was lay out plates she'd made up yesterday before Ellie, her help, had left for her own family Christmas.

"I was just watching the weather," she said, knowing that she was picking again at a scab that should be ignored. "It's terrible in Donegal."

"Good thing we're not there, then," Robert said and downed his sherry.

The strong smell of her own sherry turned her stomach. She set the glass down. The liquid sloshed, a watery sound that mocked the instinct that something was wrong – just like 40 years ago when she'd stopped still, knowing that something awful had happened. It had been hours before her parents had made her sit down while they told her the news that had dominated her life since, that her best friend had died. It was, she often feared, why she had married Robert: to stay close to Belle's family and remain part of their circle of loss.

As the first guests turned in through the gates, it occurred to Jean that she had no idea why he'd married her.

CHAPTER NINE

Lough Birds

AMELIA TRUDGED THROUGH a stand of pines, her feet heavier with each step in the deep snow. The bareness of the native trees interspersed amongst the pines seemed sinister, their twisted branches following her and Joe. She shook her head, trying to clear the headache that lingered, and told herself to stop imagining crazy things. Holly berries gave occasional flashes of red. It could not have looked more seasonal or felt more miserable.

"The Visitor's Centre can't be far," Joe said, not for the first time. His face – what she could see of it between the hat pulled down over his forehead and the collar of his coat turned up – glowed red, raw from the elements. "Unless we've got turned around."

Anyone could get turned around. Especially if they didn't know where they'd been to start with. Every part of the forest looked the same. The whole sequence of events had conspired to bring them here, so why not the trees, too? The hare kept flashing into her thoughts. How it had been on the road; how it waited until the skid happened before hopping away.

"Look on the bright side," said Joe, ever the optimist. "It's stopped snowing. So long as it stays off, the park will definitely have people here tomorrow."

Hopefully he was right. With clearer roads walkers would come out, the masochistic ones who liked hiking in harsh weather. The ones who came prepared and knew what they were doing. She hunched into her coat and trudged in Joe's shadow, tracking his footprints with her own, her hands thrust deep into her pockets for warmth. Best not to mention they had still to make it to tomorrow.

"There's something over there!" Joe's voice was thick with relief. "Look – through the trees." He broke into a shambling run, and she followed, avoiding branches that whipped back at her. She came out beside Joe on a ridge overlooking the lough.

The lough. The centre of the estate, bordered by a walkway and narrow road, both of which would be easy to follow. They weren't lost anymore; they could find their way to shelter. Cold air hit her face, coming off the water. It carried a sweet smell that promised more snow. They had not found the lough a moment too soon.

Amelia gazed across the stone-grey water, trying to make out any signs of life on the hills – smoke from a bothy, perhaps, or a car moving – but there was nothing.

"Jesus," said Joe. "That wind's strong. We'll freeze if we stay here."

"Which way?" she asked. The narrow causeway path that followed the water stretched to their right and left. She put her hand on Joe's shoulder and he, knowing the signal, bent one shoulder down. She opened the orange pouch on the front of his rucksack and took one of their mint cakes out. She broke it in two, giving him a piece, and sucked at her own. The sugar warmed in her mouth and melted. "Any idea?"

"No." Joe sounded as frustrated as she felt. "We could have come out of the woods anywhere."

She thought – from the map she'd looked at in the name of hurried research – that the castle lay at one end of the lough and the Visitors' Centre at the other. Which would be useful if she had any idea which end was which.

She went to the edge of the ridge, craning her neck to look both ways but nothing could tell her which was better. The path appeared to have been laid over bog land, following its ups and downs. But at least it was a route of some sort. She lifted her chin and caught a sense of – not rightness, exactly, but energy – coming from the left. From the right, she got nothing.

Well, a hunch was better than nothing. "That way."

They made their way down to the causeway. On another day the walk would be beautiful, through some of the wildest country Donegal, already wild, had to offer. Today, it was a misery of freezing wind, of slipping and grabbing each other, of splashing through brooks melting through the snow. On the other side of the causeway grey lough water lapped with a constant slap-slap, broken only by the occasional screech of birds.

A stab of pain in her right temple made Amelia miss her step and stumble. Joe carried on, oblivious. A flock of birds flew in from the mountains, over the lough, circling and squawking. They looked like no birds she had seen before; their bodies heavy and black, their heads thickset with beaks that were too large for their head. When one swooped low, Amelia was sure she could see a line of teeth held within the beak. Bile rose in her, a hot wash of fear. Familiar sweat broke along her brow.

"Joe…" She pointed at the sky. She didn't even know if he'd see the birds. God, she hoped he could see them. "What are they?"

The flock circled overhead, not just over the lough, but the forest too. The circle, she realised, enclosed herself and Joe.

Joe squinted, hand over his eyes. "I don't know. Ducks. Or geese. Nothing that can help us find shelter."

They weren't ducks. Or geese. The cries they gave, bitter-sharp and angry, were more human than bird and, whilst they were big enough to be swans, they didn't have long necks, but were squat and heavy. And black as night.

A howl went up, accompanying the birds' cry. Heart racing, she scanned the mountains that ringed the lough and forest. There were no wolves in the wild in Ireland. She was sure of it. The howling went up again, from another part of the mountains. She imagined she could hear a drumming, too, an insistent beating noise. Either that or it was her own heartbeat, too loud in her ears.

"Can you hear that?" she asked Joe.

"What?"

"Some kind of animal."

Joe cocked his head, listening. Another howl went up, but his posture didn't change. "Nope. Just the damn ducks." He frowned. "Are you all right? Amelia?"

She couldn't tell him. He'd never understand. He'd think she was crazy. All her family's warnings crashed around her, about not admitting any of her 'notions', for fear of the reception she'd get. Her panic gained strength, raw and undeniable, coming at her in great hammers.

"Amelia!" Joe took her shoulders, gripping her tightly. "You're scaring me."

She was scaring herself, too. The birds broke away in a great wheel, high over the forest. The howling stopped, leaving only the faint drumming that seemed to echo her restless dreams from the previous night and the pale, shaken, Joe.

"I'm okay," she said. She'd have to be; she couldn't stay on the bank of the lough, not knowing if there was something watching her. Her headache lifted and she started to walk, Joe beside her, as fast as she was able.

They turned a corner and she grabbed Joe's arm. "Look!" Ahead stood two gates, stone statues of griffins on top of on each. Beyond, a path twisted between thick foliage laden with heavy snow. After the raw-edged causeway, the path looked benign. Welcoming even. Relief made Amelia's chest light, testament to how spooked she'd been.

"We've made it." There was no mistaking the relief in Joe's voice. "Just in time. Look." He held out a gloved hand and caught a snowflake. It lay against his palm and melted, white falling to grey before vanishing. Soon, the last of the daylight would fade, as if ink were being spilled over the sky. This close to the solstice, daylight barely stayed until 4 o'clock, let alone on a snowy day. They hurried through the open gateway into the castle's tree-lined driveway, shadows falling all around them.

"Let's see if there's anyone here," said Joe. "There

might be security. In fact, this place might even have a payphone."

She doubted that but marched up the drive. A payphone would be too convenient. It would make it too easy to get away – and she didn't think the estate wanted that. Trees surrounded her on either side. The path no longer felt benign but closed in, leading them to the heart of somewhere. She could not shake the feeling that it might not be shelter they had found, but a trap. The snow began to fall more heavily again, giving no option but to go forwards, deeper into the driveway leading to the castle and gardens.

CHAPTER TEN
Home Truths

"HONESTLY, ROBERT! I *knew* you'd be fascinated!"

Jean tensed at Alice McAllister's shrill voice and she hated that she did. She should rise above Alice and trust that Robert had better taste. Except that Alice's hand lay on Robert's sleeve and she was looking up at him, mouth open, almost breathless in her focus on him. He leaned into her, smiling, eyes meeting hers, and Jean couldn't tell if it was the perfect host's smile or something more.

Alice kept in good shape, a Pilates class every Wednesday, yoga on a Friday. Her top was artlessly low so that the swell of her breasts was impossible to miss. She put her head back and laughed, as if Robert were the most entertaining thing in the dining room. "It was the talk of the town, poor Sam dying like that. So sudden. He was so active. The funeral was huge, but that's not the best of it." A snort of laughter reminded Jean of one of the mares. "It was claimed the Grey Lady made an appearance – a banshee of all things! You do have to wonder at how crazy people can be."

Jean hurried over, cheese plate in hand, ready to interrupt the conversation. Too late – Alice was in full voice.

"Apparently some artist captured its likeness. In fact –" Alice glanced over at Jean, eyes shining. "– did I hear that she had been out to visit with yourselves? Something about a commission to paint a picture. She asked directions in the village and Isobel, in the shop, recognised her name from the newspaper – they did a little feature on the supposed banshee. You know how they fill up column inches with any old rubbish."

"Indeed," said Robert. He met Jean's eyes and his own were cold. "Imagine us commissioning someone like that. I'm surprised you didn't hear about any of this, Jean."

A slight emphasis on her name gave just an indication of his annoyance. Alice glanced between them, taking in the atmosphere. Her nostrils flared in what might have been anticipated triumph.

"Well, Newcastle is a little away," she said. "And I'm sure Jean would have dismissed such silly talk, even if she had been in the loop. To be honest, I think it was the drama of the death. These things take hold and become gossip."

"That's true," said Robert. "Ideas do, indeed, sometimes take a hold."

The subtext was clear. Ideas like Jean's belief that something untoward had happened to Belle, even though everyone in the estate at the time refuted that. Robert, who had found the body, insisted her suspicions had no basis. The Gardai had confirmed his story at the time. Her own

Private Investigator had turned up nothing new, but only added more questions. The only thing she had to base her suspicions on were her dreams, full of Belle's accusations.

She faced her husband, and he her. Neither looked away. Robert would not back down; he would be furious at what he'd perceive as a betrayal. She kept her own head up, unashamed. Perhaps she should have told him about Amelia, but he would never have allowed her to commission the painting and he held the ace card; she'd married his money, not him into hers.

The society voices trailed away as the knowledge something was wrong sunk in. A score of gossips waited, delighted at this bonus on Christmas day: strife between the Sweeneys, of all people. Jean knew she should turn away, refill glasses, do anything to save face, but she didn't. This – Belle – had lain between her and Robert for forty years. At some point, it had to be faced.

Robert composed himself quicker than she did. Years of hiding his emotions had given him that ability. Her twenty-five year marriage made her a mere amateur in comparison.

He inclined his head to Alice. "How fascinating. Now, please, excuse me. I must see to my other guests. It's been lovely catching up, as always."

In the hall a child yelled at another, something about eating his dust, breaking the long, still moment. Jean forced a smile onto her face. "I'll just organise dessert."

The room relaxed. Voices started up again. The crack was once again hidden under manners.

"So much food, as ever! I don't know how I'll ever eat again today," said Alice's husband Michael, a man so banal

Jean often felt that walls had more to offer.

"But we shall," said Alice in her brittle voice. She would have her turkey in the oven and her table set. The best crystal would be shining, the expensive crackers handpicked to match the room. A Christmas morning gathering would not be allowed to dent her endeavours. "I see the morning as the warm up, really."

She gave the smile of a cat who thinks it has done something clever without knowing what it might be, and swept from the room, her damage complete.

CHAPTER ELEVEN
The Folly

AMELIA REACHED THE end of the driveway, where it opened onto a tarmac circle in front of what appeared to be a castle, complete with turrets and balustrades. A small castle, to be fair, but still several storeys high and finished with castellated details and a turret. A rich person's folly was the last thing she'd expected to find, buried within the mountains like a secret encased in this barren land.

The snow on the path to the front of the castle was unbroken, although bird tracks were visible at the edges. Soon, only the looped chain-barrier would mark where the path began and ended.

A caw from the trees behind made Amelia turn and search through the deep forest. Did the birds from the lough roost in the estate? Perhaps they'd been in the estate all day, waiting for her and Joe. Goosebumps rose along her arms. She wanted to turn back, find the car miraculously intact, and get the hell out of this place.

"Civilisation!" shouted Joe. He shrugged off his

backpack and thrust his arms aloft like a Hollywood hero who'd saved the day. He swooped in a circle on the castle's courtyard. "We're saved!"

His antics forced a laugh Amelia didn't think she had in her. Joe had obviously noticed nothing sinister. Whatever had been over the lough – if there had even been something – had no home here, in this sheltered estate.

"Well, nearly civilisation," she teased. "Some people would be nice."

He mimicked taking a bullet to his chest. "You wound me. I give you bricks. And indoor toilets!"

God, yes, the toilet. She'd had to go once on the way through the woods, pulling down her trousers and tights, pee steaming in the cold air, the acrid smell of it, the quick pull up of her clothes before her butt froze. She didn't fancy having to go again.

"Right, then. Let's go rouse the cavalry." Joe didn't mention the lack of footprints in the snow, either here or on the causeway path. Surely the place wouldn't be left unstaffed, even on Christmas Day? The public estate's grounds were never closed. She hurried forwards. The shadows cast by the grey walls were long around her.

She reached the door, almost skiteing on the iced-over front stoop, and tried its handle. It didn't move. She tried it again, pushing harder, but still nothing happened and a glance through a narrow side window showed no sign of life.

"Nothing," she said. It wasn't fair. They'd made it to the castle. They deserved to find help.

"There must be someone," said Joe. "Security, at least."

He hit the heel of his hand against the door, dull thud after dull thud. "Hello!" His words echoed round the courtyard. "Anyone home!?"

The last of the sun sank behind the tower, deepening the cold air. Amelia crossed her arms over her chest and rubbed them.

"Can we find another way in?" she asked, teeth chattering. If it was this cold now, how much worse would it be overnight? "Break a window, maybe?"

"We could try that. I'm willing to take the rap," said Joe. "I doubt they'd throw the book at us, given the circumstances."

She didn't care what it took. They needed shelter. Joe's tent would be useless against this kind of cold. She spotted a branch, half-sheltered from the snow. She crunched over the turning circle to pick it up but it *was* damp, after all. But thick, with a good weight to it.

"Go ahead," Joe said. "They'll thank us. They'll only be able to reclaim damages if we're not popsicles."

Amelia ignored the joke. She marched up to the small window beside the door and took aim. She hit the glass square on, so hard that the branch recoiled in her hand, but the window didn't break.

"Here, let me try," said Joe. He took the branch from her and swung it, holding nothing back. It hit the window but, again, the glass didn't break. "Shit." Joe hit it again and a splintering noise made her think it had worked, but it was the branch that had shattered in Joe's hands. The window remained undamaged.

"Christ. We could be all night at this." Joe stepped back. "Give me some space." He kicked solidly at the door, but it didn't give. He tried again, and again, face red with effort.

Amelia grabbed his arm. "It's not going to give. It's a castle. The door's probably half a foot thick."

"Fuck." Joe bent his head back as he took in the building. "No balcony? Anything?"

"We could try round the back."

"You're right." Joe lifted his rucksack with a low groan. "Next time, I'll just pack a body and have done with it."

"I'll take it," she said.

He ignored her and she knew better than to push. Joe would be blaming himself for crashing the car and stranding them here. He didn't cope well with letting people down. Allowing him to carry the rucksack would go some way to making him feel better.

She followed him away from the castle. Her eyes scanned the treeline, the path, the darkly shaded areas, but nothing moved.

"This might be worth a look at," said Joe, his hand already pushing on a metal gate. Amelia hesitated before walking through, not liking the high walls that surrounded the garden stretching from the back of the castle.

Joe glanced up at the sky. "There has to be somewhere we could use in a garden this size."

"You'd think so." A grid of square pathways of smooth snow were broken up by orderly beds of plants huddled into white, uneven bumps.

Amelia hurried up the path, keeping her distance from the encircling walls. She passed a second gate and stopped long enough to pop her head through. Another path led into a formal garden framed by shrouded terraces. Once again, no footprints broke the snow on the path, although there were hoof prints just visible in the falling darkness. A paw print, just the right size for a hare, was clearer. A warning prickle crawled up her spine. One movement and she'd be off, not caring where she went.

"Bingo!" Joe's voice carried from the walled garden. "I think we're saved!"

"Really?!" She took a last look at the prints – *they were big for deer, weren't they?* – and hurried to where Joe waited in front of a small cottage. A low wall surrounded it and on its gate a plaque announced it as the Gardener's Cottage, although there was no sign of life in it. She supposed the head gardener lived somewhere else these days.

"There's a chimney," she said. Thinking of a fire brought home how cold she was: even through her layers, the cold had seeped into her bones. "It looks pretty sturdy."

"Let's hope the door is a little more co-operative." Joe pushed the gate and it opened easily. Part of the wall behind the cottage had crumbled, leaving a gash that led into the terraced garden, which looked wild and tangled, away from the formal lawn.

"Useful short cut when we head back to the car park," said Joe.

Amelia hurried up the short path. She turned the handle, hoping their luck would change, but no; the door was locked.

"Right. That's it." Joe dropped his rucksack and put his shoulder to the door. It didn't budge. He stepped back and kicked, once, twice, and then a third time. "Come on, you bastard." He shouldered the door once more and the wood splintered. Another kick gave enough space to clamber through.

"Ladies first," said Joe.

She ducked past him, turning sideways to fit through the crack. She stopped to rip some of the splinters free, making room for the taller Joe. He passed her the rucksack and then followed her in.

"Well," he said, hands on hips. "It's shelter."

Amelia felt around the door and found the cold, hard square of a lightswitch. She flicked it, not expecting it to work, but lights came on either side of the hallway. "Bingo."

She stepped into the room on her right. Fluorescent tubes flickered but stayed on. The walls were lined with pictures depicting the estate's grounds and gardens, with information panels below each one. Several display desks held more information: notes about the garden and copies of plans. One picture, of a dark outdoor pool overlooking the lough, took her attention. The water lay dark and still, as if holding secrets within it. A single lily pad broke the surface. She moved closer and read its inscription: *The Lido. 1945.*

"Hallelujah!" Joe's voice came from the next room, breaking her concentration, and she realised her shoulders were tight with tension. "We have a kettle! And tea bags. And custard creams! It's Christmas!"

It was, she remembered. Sometime in the future they'd laugh about today. It would become part of the story of their relationship – the Christmas they got stranded in

Donegal. She turned away from the forever-still picture and headed to the far end of the second, similarly laid-out, room. Her boots echoed dully as she walked.

At the back of the room, in the small kitchen, Joe had the kettle on. They waited the endless wait for it to boil. She'd never needed something hot inside her so badly.

Night fell as they drank their tea, washing down more of the mint cake, alternated with a custard cream. If they'd been able to carry more food from the car, they'd have been well fixed but, for now, the mint cake would have to do. Outside, the snow continued to fall. Amelia dreaded to think how deep it would be by morning but at least they had shelter and lights. There was even a small toilet. One way or another, they'd survive the night. If they got a fire going, it might even be cosy. Amelia should be grateful. But, mostly, as she watched the snow falling, she was scared.

CHAPTER TWELVE
An Awkward Admission

JEAN WISHED CHRISTMAS dinner was the highlight of her day, like Alice's. She found herself envying Ellie, her help, spending Christmas dinner with her parents in their council house. Anything would be better than just her and Robert, and the cold silence.

She set the M&S turkey crown on the table. The roast was small, almost shabby. The expensive crackers, chosen to match the heavy linen, lay unpulled. Beside her place setting, the phone waited for her to try, once again, to reach Donegal, her worry growing with each extra hour.

Robert carved the crown – more slicing than carving, really. He set two thin pieces on her plate, and several on his own. Perhaps making a point about her non-existent need to diet or, more likely, comparing her to Alice. He knew that was the sort of thing she would take to heart. Determinedly, she speared another two slices and set them on her plate before helping herself to veg and roast potatoes.

"So, when were you going to tell me?" Robert slopped

gravy over his turkey.

"Tell you what?" But she knew, of course.

"Please don't pretend to be stupid, Jean. I assume you've commissioned this woman to go to Donegal? No doubt you want her to prod around your obsession about Belle."

"I didn't think you would approve." She stabbed a potato with her fork, as if mutilating a vegetable might make her feel better. "I thought it would be better to see what, if anything, Amelia King might turn up first."

"I don't approve." He took a gulp of wine, not savouring the good bottle as he normally would. All this slovenliness was supposed to annoy her. She had gone to such pains with the dinner, making sure the wine was just-so and the table exquisite; slopping and slurping were designed to put her teeth on edge. She forced a smile, knowing it would rankle if he couldn't upset her.

"Because I shouldn't open old wounds?" she said. "I thought you'd understand. Belle was your sister, after all. Surely you mourn her? Even a little."

"She was and I do. But she's been dead forty years." Robert set his fork down and leaned forwards. His muscles bunched under his shirt, smoothing the material over his chest and along his arms. "There is nothing to find out about Belle's death." His cheek flexed. "We have been over this and over this. No one has ever found anything, whatsoever, to suggest things were different than I found them. Not even your damned detective."

"He said—"

"He said nothing useful. Certainly not enough to justify his fee. Belle drowned. It was an icy day, the paving around the lido was treacherous and she slipped. The cold water would have taken the breath from her. She drowned in moments, Jean. Without calling out and without anyone seeing anything, hearing anything, or doing anything to her." His hand clenched. "Can I make that any clearer to you?"

"But *how* did it happen?" Jean said. "Belle didn't like ice. Why did she go to the lido? The police report said the ice around it was lethal." And that was before she even got started onto the shoddy autopsy, and the hints that Robert's father had paid the Gardai to speed things up and close the case quickly.

"I. Don't. Know."

"But I *need* to know." Could he hear the pleading in her voice? If he did, he didn't respond to it, or answer any of the discrepancies. There had been no water in Belle's lungs, which meant she had been dead before she hit the pool. A small crack in her skull had been recorded, and then reference to it removed from the report. If it had existed, had it been done at the time, or in an earlier fall from the tree Robert had told their parents about? Had someone taken trusting Belle? Robert's mother remembered hearing howling nearby but a dog had never been found.

The black hole of knowledge ate at Jean. Her last memory of Belle was etched in her mind. Belle in her red coat, waving from the back seat of the over-filled car as they'd left the village. Jean had waved back without knowing that they'd never see each other again. She could have convinced her mother to let Belle stay, if she'd known. Mrs Sweeney, Belle's mother, wouldn't have liked it, snob that she was. She had looked down on Jean's childhood home, even though it had been comfortable and clean and welcoming. But Belle could have convinced her, given how difficult things were in the Sweeney family that year. She should have kept Belle safe, with her. The endless guilt never left, but instead ate at her insides.

"I have to know," she said, again, hating that she sounded petulant when she wasn't.

"Not this way." Robert snorted. "A psychic artist? What were you thinking of? And how much did you agree to pay her, to buy into this?"

"I didn't tell her why I wanted her to go," said Jean. "I'm not that stupid."

"How much?" he asked. Robert would not let it go. He never did.

"Five thousand," she said.

"And then the rest. You can tell her the deal is off." Robert pushed his plate away, his dinner barely touched, and scraped his chair back. "What makes you believe this story about the banshee anyway? You must know it's gossip."

"I don't think it is," she said. If a lie wouldn't work, perhaps the truth would be better. He'd guessed most of it anyway. Jean pushed a piece of turkey around her plate, with no stomach to eat it. "I spoke to one of the people in Newcastle that day, and he was sure she'd seen the banshee. In fact..." *In for a penny, in for a pound.* At least she might be able to convince him her reasoning had been sound and he would know she hadn't done it as some sort of crazy lady. That she had some *evidence*. "Here." She fished her phone from her pocket and brought up the picture of the harbour. She pointed to the figure on the quayside. "Do you see that woman?"

"Yes. So what?"

"That's the banshee," she said. She held a hand up before Robert could interrupt and denigrate her words. "Hear me out. No one else saw the woman that day. But the man who died heard the banshee. Now, I checked everything I could about that particular banshee." She held up her fingers and started to check them off. "It always appears at the harbour. It comes in the form of a lady dressed in grey who appears to walk on or near the edge of the water." She paused. "Robert, banshees are normally only heard at the death of people in one family. The man was *from* that family, my sources say. An old Newcastle family. He is legitimate. Amelia is not."

"So?"

"So she *saw* the banshee. She is sensitive. But, also… look at the picture. Look at the way she has captured the place. Can't you feel there is something there that she had sensed? Can't you see it? She sees the layers of a place." She took her phone back and brought up the Ballygally picture. "And she sees ghosts."

He didn't respond. Perhaps he hadn't understood.

"Robert," she said. "She could see Belle. Surely that's worth a few thousand pounds?"

Robert didn't respond. She wasn't sure how to deal with his silence. Anger, she'd have faced. Being mocked would have been nothing more than another blow, worth it if Amelia discovered the truth of Belle's death.

"Anyway," she said, setting her own fork down. She was damned if he'd belittle her by ignoring her. "You're too late to stop things. She's already there."

"Where?" His hand tightened around his napkin.

"In Donegal. In the cottage. She's going to paint Glenveagh in winter."

"She is in Donegal now? Have you seen the weather? Anything could happen to her." He got to his feet. "And she doesn't know why you've sent her? Jesus. Have you spoken to her today?"

Worry wormed through Jean's body, tightening her chest. "No. I think the phones are probably down."

"You're sure she sees ghosts?"

"Yes."

"And supernatural beings?" His questions were scatter-gun quick.

"It appears so." She ran her hands through her hair. "Why does this matter, Robert? She's not on her own. She has her boyfriend with her."

"Her boyfriend?" Robert's face drained of all colour. He leant his hands on the table, fists clenched. His forearms were corded, his neck tight. "Get your coat. We're going."

"What? Where?" He was making no sense, and Robert always made sense. Cold sense, often bordering on the mean, but still sense.

"Glenveagh."

"*You*?" Robert hadn't even gone to Donegal when his mother's ashes had been scattered at the last place she'd shared with her daughter. "You swore you'd never go back. And what about the weather?"

"The weather doesn't matter," he said, and his eyes were bleak. "If what you say is true, the weather isn't what they have to fear."

"Well, what then?" she asked. "You told me nothing happened!"

"Get your coat," he said. "Either that, or I'll go alone."

She would never know what happened. She would go through the rest of her life wondering if her husband was the murderer she feared he might be.

"I'll come."

She did the unthinkable. She left a room full of uncleared food, the dishes unwashed, and followed her husband out into the cold night to drive to Donegal, into a white-out.

CHAPTER THIRTEEN
The First Circle

AMELIA HUDDLED INTO her coat. It might be more sheltered than the garden, but the cottage was still cold, especially with the gashed front door.

"Right, then," said the relentlessly cheerful Joe. "We need to sort out a fire." He pointed at a boarded-up fireplace. "You get that opened up and the tinder ready and I'll get wood. There has to be some down at the big house."

"We should both go," she said, hating the idea of going back into the garden. Now darkness had fallen, she dreaded what might – or might not be, depending on her imagination – waiting.

"No, you get the fire prepared," said Joe. "Otherwise, it'll be longer until we can heat up." He gave a light smile. "I'll be careful out there, don't worry. It's not like there're any muggers hiding in corners."

He pulled his scarf up and his hat down, returning to the nose-and-eyes look of earlier, and side-stepped through the broken door. He passed the window a moment later, and vanished into the darkness.

The cottage was quiet without him. The lights burned brightly, shining out in the garden, but they were harsh, not comforting. Distracting herself, Amelia checked through the kitchen cupboards. An industrial-sized pack of napkins and some paper plates. A pair of desiccated dishcloths lay in the back of the under-sink cupboard. Enough to get a fire started, perhaps, but she'd need wood. Whatever Joe found might be damp. In fact, knowing their luck, the woodpile's cover would have blown off and everything would be soaked.

She went back into the main room. She couldn't bring herself to burn any of the archive material, although there was plenty of it, but the wooden frames on the picture and display cases might be worth raiding. She took a frame down, prying the wood free, all the time checking that the doorway was still empty, her ears alert for any movement.

At last she forced the plywood back from the frame. The pane fell out and she jumped back with a yell, but it was plastic and didn't break. She snapped open a row of frames, making a reasonable pile of kindling in the middle of the floor.

Now for the fire. She knelt by the boarded-up section and gave it a rap, hoping the chimney hadn't been bricked in. A hollow echo came back. It could have been the cottage replying, so clear was the thud.

The join where the fireplace had been closed off was neat, with sharp, clean edges. Whoever had carried out the job had done so with care, taking no chances that the chimney would be easily uncovered. She tried forcing the corners of the join, hoping for a weakness, but there was none, so she fell back on Joe's policy of kicking things, drawing her leg back to get some decent force into it. She gave the wall a boot, and another. It felt strangely cathartic, taking out the day's frustration.

On the fourth kick, the seam on the right gave, revealing a gap. She knelt and, with some twisting and a fair bit of cursing, managed to pry her fingers around the wood. She pulled with all her might, bending one nail right back. The wood was not ply or balsa, but a solid piece of hard wood, much more than sealing a fireplace would require.

She forced more of her hand to gain purchase. It crushed her fingers between wall and wood, and her wrist flared in pain but, with gritted teeth, she prised the board further forward.

It came away with a suddenness that sent her falling onto her arse. Dust chased her fall, black and smelling of age. A flash of pain crossed her forehead; a white light across her eyes. Sweat broke, cold along her spine.

She stared at the hole, sure something would emerge. *She was not alone.* The familiar tightness in her chest came, warning her that *something* was happening. She closed her eyes, willing this to be nothing more than panic.

A pile of soot fell from the chimney into the grate, landing with a puff of black dust that became a thin line, like tendrils reaching for her. It didn't have the acrid smell of fire, but something older, almost earth-like. She shrank back but couldn't have said what from.

The soot dissipated. Her headache lifted and she was able to draw a proper breath. The fireplace stood before her, uncovered and benign.

"Get a grip, Amelia," she said, but the words caught in her throat, twisted and tight. She staggered to her feet. *Nothing there, see? Nothing at all.* She turned to the hallway, with its shattered door. *Nor there. Just my twisted imagination.*

Determinedly, she picked up the pictures from her plundered frames, ensuring she lined each up with the last and handled them as little as possible. Some were original cuttings, not copies, and she didn't want to stain them. She forced herself to focus on the moment, how each piece of paper felt different, how the older cuttings were thicker than the modern copies and felt more substantial. The damage to the door she could live with, and the fireplace could be easily sealed up again, but ruining the carefully-gathered history would be wrong. Some dated back to the 19th century, covering some sort of atrocity that had happened during the famine, and she wondered if that was what she was feeling: a residue from an ancient horror.

She piled the papers in the corner of the next room, well away from the fireplace and any smoke it might give. From the top picture, a child stared at her, strangely familiar.

A dead child, the headline said, found in the lido by her brother on a freezing winter's day. Amelia checked the date and saw the newspaper was just a day off forty years old. She sank onto her haunches, reading through it. The child's name had been Belle and she had been ten. Something tugged at Amelia's memory, something elusive, but the link wouldn't come. Her headache returned, a quiet throb caused by the long day and the cold, and nothing would bring the memory to mind.

A noise from behind made Amelia spin around. Too late, it occurred to her that the bright lights would tell anyone – or anything – that the cottage was occupied, not just Joe.

The noise came again, a low snuffling. Amelia set Belle's picture down and forced herself to walk towards the hall, ignoring her shaking legs.

"Who's there?" she asked. "Joe? Is that you?"

Surely he would have announced himself, not freaked her out? She stopped at the doorway. Her heart hammered, and her palms were sweaty. She braced to run, or to fight, whatever it took.

The noise came again, still in the hallway; the only way out of the cottage. She had let herself become trapped.

Deciding it was better to take the initiative, Amelia drew a deep breath and, with a '*hai*!' jumped into the hall, ready to barrel her way out of the door.

A small fox yelped and turned tail, disappearing like liquid gold in the darkness.

"Jesus." She leaned against the wall. Her legs shook so much she thought they might give beneath her. She pushed herself away from the wall and towards the front door. She might have overreacted to the noise but Joe should be back by now. He was an experienced hill walker, who knew that shelter was ultimately more important than a fire.

She stuck her head through the gash in the door and into a raw, freezing wind. The garden, beyond the light from the windows, was utterly dark, but seemed still. She comforted herself that the fox would not have come near the cottage if anything had been around it.

"Joe...?" She cleared her throat. She didn't want to step outside. She wanted him to hear her and call back and things to be okay. "Joe!"

Her voice disappeared into the night, as if snatched. A moment later, she thought she heard an answering call, high pitched, not quite like Joe. She paused to listen and it came again and this time she thought it might be him. He might have fallen. He might need help.

With a deep breath, she stepped out.

CHAPTER FOURTEEN
The Watchers

AMELIA MARCHED – as best she could on the snow, but the intent was there – down the cottage's path, towards the low wall that divided it from the walled garden. Moonlight shone; it seemed for now the snow had finished falling, and wasn't that convenient with them already trapped? The garden stood silent. Beyond its surrounding walls, the formal garden and woods waited. Gardens within gardens, walls within walls, all enclosing her and Joe within their centre. The thought felt important but elusive, almost slippery.

Amelia put her hand on the low wall and clambered over. There were no signs of Joe's footprints despite the pause in snowfall. She hesitated, torn between going back and the thought of Joe lying hurt somewhere. In the end, concern for him won over her fear and, feeling like the heroine in a bad slasher movie, she made her way down the moonlit path, towards the castle and its long conservatory. She stayed close to the high surrounding wall. Even in its shelter, she felt exposed. Anything could be perched in the trees beyond, or on the castle's roof, and she wouldn't know. The dark birds from the lake could be watching her; the hare from earlier waiting to catch her again. Chill air stole through her clothes, making her tremble.

A sound made her stop. Her breath frosted white as she stood, still, listening. Rhythmic beats and what sounded like a half-muted horn, as if from her dream the night before. She was sure they were coming from the formal gardens. Instinctively, she looked back. The lights from the cottage shone out, beckoning her to return to the only safety there might be. She might have turned back except, suddenly, a yell came. One she knew.

"Joe!" She sped down the path, not caring about the ice and snow. She reached the gate that opened into the formal gardens and turned into it. Her legs went one way and her momentum carried her the other. For a heart-stopping moment she felt sure she was falling, but caught herself on the edge of the archway's brickwork and skidded to a halt in its shadows.

The silence around her felt broken; the garden too still.

A sound came, to her right, and above. Not Joe but the shuffling of something moving. The sound was muffled. Sneaky. Instinct made her pull further into the shadow of the archway which she'd almost burst through a moment before.

The sound came again, from somewhere above her. One of the displays in the cottage had shown a maze of terraced gardens overlooking the central lawn, all interlinking with each other, connected by narrow pathways and stairs. If she passed through the gate, she could be walking into a trap.

She craned her head, trying to work out what lay around the gate. To her right, it was open to the lawn but shrubbery lined the path to the left. Slowly, softly, she moved towards it. She barely breathed, sure any noise would be the end of her; whatever lurked in the shadows would be as attuned to her as she was it.

Steady, steady. She juked out from the archway, just as she had earlier in the day. A thick rhododendron reached almost all the way to the stone wall. She dropped onto all fours and crawled, ignoring the freezing wetness that seeped through to her knees, using the shrub to cover her progress. She stayed down until she was at the back of the rhododendron. She'd once watched a kitten hunt a bird using the depths of a hawthorne bush for safety, and tried to move like the cat had, each movement part of a whole that didn't draw attention.

A shallow rivulet caught her out, and she splashed into it. She drew her breath in a sharp gasp, but the stream also provided the opportunity to follow its path through undergrowth, sheltering her movements from the garden. She crept as far as she could, into a dense tangle of overhanging brambles, and then crouched in the shrubbery beside the stream, listening.

No sound came. She began to think she was imagining everything, that the whole night – hearing Joe scream, feeling watched – was only her overactive imagination. She was almost at the point of believing it would be okay to step out when something whirred overhead, a beat-beat of wings carrying a musty smell akin to that of the cottage's fireplace.

Amelia ducked from it. Her heart pounded so hard she could hear it, thick in her ears.

"Come and play!" The cracked voice came from the other side of the garden "We have a toy."

A scream followed. Long, pained and human, and definitely Joe. Amelia's hands clenched, wanting to fight, but she stayed her ground. If she allowed herself to be found, it would be over for both of them. Whatever *it* was. She waited long minutes, and then squeezed through the shrubbery, crouching low, to where she could see the garden.

Three figures moved towards the gate to the walled garden, caught in the sharp moonlight. Tall and muscular, their skin leathered and old, they looked less like an animal than a creature which had forgotten how to be human.

They loped across the lawn, covering it at an astonishing speed. When they reached the gate, they paused, sniffing the air. One homed in on where she'd stood, scant minutes before. It lifted its head, taking in the garden and the pathway. It came close to where she'd splashed into the stream, then stopped and went back to the gateway, sniffing again. At last, the creatures left through the arch.

A moment later, a long howl went up, no doubt picking up her scent in the garden. Hounds streamed down from the terraces, all haunches and loose-muscled fur. Behind them came more of the leathered creatures, some on foot but others, joining the pack from further down the garden as if formed from the darkness, on great black horses that snorted danger.

The creatures flowed out of the gate in a cascade of hooves and fur, hunting horns blaring. As they passed, Amelia realised the mounts weren't horses. They were too sharp in shape. Their legs were muscular and bunched, part canine, part racehorse. Their eyes rolled red, wide and fearless. When one nickered, it wasn't the sound of a horse but something lower, akin to a growl.

The garden fell quiet as the hunt – because that's what it was, a hunt in a moonlit garden that made no sense – left. In the walled garden, hooves beat and horns mingled with yells, but in the terraced garden all was still.

Why hadn't the creatures already searched for her beyond the terraced garden? They had not checked the fully-lit cottage. Instead, the fox had drawn her out. Something important nagged at her, but she didn't know what it was.

She straightened into a low crouch. The hunt would not stay away forever. She stayed near the shrubbery, but walked into something hard, buried in the bushes. She came up onto her toes, and bit down a yell just in time.

A statue stared back at her, some kind of Balinese goddess, both ugly and strangely beautiful. Amelia laid her hand on it. *If you really are a goddess, let you be a kind one. If so, a little help would be good.* She gulped and set off, creeping to the back of a long pavilion that formed one edge of the lawn. There, she paused.

A path to her left led towards the lough, no doubt taking her onto the causeway they'd followed earlier. Could she head that way and lure the creatures away from Joe? She could double back to the garden later. But that wouldn't work: she'd be exposed and easy to track. Indeed, she suspected it was what they wanted. The horns, the beating hooves, the taunting words and screams, all convinced her this was about sport and they'd be happy for her to provide it.

Decided, she crept to the right until, at last, a path came into sight, following the line of the lawn. On it lay Joe, his eyes open and shining.

Alive. The flood of relief made Amelia's head spin, but ebbed when she took in the detail. He was pinned between two of the creatures. She blinked, perhaps hoping to clear the illusion, but they were still. She'd never experienced something like this before. Odd sensations, yes. A vision of something barely there, as at Ballygally. Even the glimpse of a spirit, like at the harbour at Newcastle. But never a repeating image. And never with such a strong feeling coming from it, a blackness of spirit, a primeval sense of something both familiar and terribly wrong.

Joe glared up at them. One of his trouser legs had been torn, the skin beneath raked with a long cut – she assumed that had been the reason for his screams. She stared, weighing up her chances of freeing him, but pulled back. What could she do against the monsters? They were real, not something to be dismissed.

She drew in a deep breath. They were real, and here, and needed to be faced. There was nothing else for it. And no one else to do it.

CHAPTER FIFTEEN
The Terraces

AMELIA STAYED CROUCHED, close to the ground. She strained her eyes, trying to make out more detail in the darkness. The creature was pressing on Joe's chest with long, almost finger-like claws.

The second monster leaned close to Joe's face. Joe mumbled something, but the sound came out thin and wheezed, as if the creature was stealing the breath from him. Would he regain it, or had they taken it forever? Was she already too late?

She couldn't be. She brought her hand up to push her hood back, the better to see, but stopped at the sight of her toggle, swinging so that its plastic coating caught the moonlight.

If the creatures who had passed her were hunters, were Joe's two guardians hunters as well? They were a pack – surely all would hunt when they could? She twisted off first one toggle, then the other. Quietly, she reached into her pocket and drew out the contents: a used tissue; a sweet that had been in there since the year dot; a lip balm she had previously thought she'd lost…

She pushed back into the undergrowth, allowing the trees and bushes to give way to her weight, as if absorbing her. If the guards noticed, with luck they'd think she was an animal. Carefully, picking her way between branches, she crept back to where the stream broadened out. Just ahead, it ran through a tunnel cut into a brick bridge where set of stone steps led to the top.

She stopped at the edge of the stream. A rustle to her left brought her head – slowly and carefully – around, but it was only the breeze shifting a bamboo patch. She counted five and darted into the darkness of the tunnel below the bridge, just about keeping her balance on the iced-over bank.

Under the shadow of the bridge, she slid into the stream mouth opening in a quiet gasp at the cold. The clack of a cobble underfoot threatened to give her away. Her heart leaped to somewhere around her ears and she pulled further into the tunnel.

Lord only knew what was around her. Rats she could live with, or any other earth creatures. What itched at her, making her want to leave the tunnel and stand where she could watch around her, was the thought of one of the monsters crouching, troll-like, behind her. She could imagine its heavy hand on her shoulder, the strength belying its bone-thin flesh. The water washed around her boots and found its way through the lace eyelets. She began to shiver and clenched her teeth against the cold, knowing their chattering would give her away.

A shadow passed the mouth of the tunnel and she hunched down, making herself as small as she could. Her butt was only inches above the water; if she overbalanced, she'd be in the stream. The shadow stopped. So did her breath. She heard – or imagined – a sniff. Her hands were clenched, ready for the shadow to come at her. She had no idea what she'd do if it did.

At last the shadow moved away. Amelia made herself count to thirty before she stepped out from the tunnel, staying close to the stone entrance. Any noise she made would be covered by the stream's snow-fed rush. She hoped.

A tree branch stretched over the water, reaching to the steps. It was thinner than she'd like, but would have to do. She reached up, numb hands closing on the wood, slippery with ice. This was a bad idea. Sadly, it was also her only idea.

She counted three under her breath. With a surge she swung upwards, bringing her legs as high as she could. She swung forwards, then back, feet scrabbling for purchase on the stonework. Her right hand slipped. She kicked with her feet, swinging again, seeking momentum. The noise being made could not be ignored, or blamed on an animal. This had been her single chance, and she wasn't going to make it past the first moment.

The heel of her boot caught on a stone parapet at the top of the staircase and battled with the branch's velocity. For a sickening moment, she thought she would fall and surely be caught by whatever waited, but managed to hook her other foot over the stone. She dived forwards. At any moment the branch would spring back and take her with it. Her knees snagged on the stonework, but her momentum carried her forwards, to tumble onto a platform at the bottom of a second flight of steps.

A juddering pain shot through each limb but at least she had landed *and* had left no footprints to show where she was. Ignoring a protest from her right knee, Amelia scrambled up the stairs and around a corner at the top. She crouched behind a stone wall that surrounded a plant-enveloped platform. That platform led onto a terraced walkway above the gardens, but she had no idea which part of the garden, too turned around by the steps and paths, and half-hidden terraces.

Using the shadows, she crept to where she could look down on Joe. One creature had left its guard position but, damn it, the other remained. It was just below her, barely five feet away. She hardly breathed. If it heard her it would be up the terrace in moments.

She tried to place the other creature, but couldn't until a slight movement near the bridge drew her attention. There it was, in the shadows of the tree whose branch she'd used. Her hands tightened around the edge of the stone parapet. She knew of no other way down; they'd trapped her.

The creature at the bridge was on its knees, head close to the ground. Smelling for her? Blood pounded in her ears. What must be its leg extended beyond the tree's shadow, across the snow-covered path. It was unbelievably long, twice that of Joe's. Could it sense her, so close? Would her smell drift down to it? Would the monster bound up the stairs with a sudden leap that she wasn't ready for, hands grasping for her?

At last, it turned away. Her breath threatened to leave in a whoosh of relief but she contained it, allowing it to trickle out as the creature passed beneath. It headed into a deeper plant-covered section of the garden, no doubt carrying out a patrol. She waited until it was out of sight and dropped her first toggle, which landed on the soft snow at the side of the path, a dark dot in the whiteness.

She stayed low behind the wall, moving in short bursts, back towards the bridge. Twice she stopped and reached down with her lip balm to smear it on the wall. Job done, she returned to close to where Joe lay, one tier below, still held by the creature who gripped both his arms as if Joe had been fighting to get free.

There were layers in this garden, terraces dropping onto the next, steps connecting each level, mazes of stone and ferns, of brambles and half-hidden paths. More layers, within the circles of the garden. She bet the garden plans might have revealed something, a secret shape in the original designs, but it was too late to find out – the creatures would be through the little cottage in their search for her.

She waited directly above Joe. The remaining creature's fingers dug into his skin.

Amelia threw the second toggle, making sure it landed on the path that led to the stream and stairs. It fell with nothing more than a tinkle but the air was so still, it could have been a bell. The monster turned its head. With a snarl it lunged for the toggle and picked it up with fingers that were long and graceful. It brought the toggle to its nose. Whatever these creatures were, they weren't clumsy, or careless, but clever. Almost human.

It rolled the toggle under its nose before raising its head and letting out a guttural cry that bore no comparison to the teasing voice from earlier. A second cry came from further in the garden. The creature below pounced on the second toggle, further along the path. That sent it off at a run; sure it had pinpointed its prey.

One chance. Just one. Amelia jumped down, her knee buckling as she landed.

"Joe!" She got a hand under his back, another on his collar, and dragged him into a seated position. "Are you hurt?"

"Cold." His teeth tapped out the word. He scrambled backwards, eyes flicking from side to side. "There are things in the garden, Amelia. Creatures." He grabbed her arm. "We need to get out of here."

A howl went up, a calling back of the pack. The two creatures must have picked up her trail; whether the false or real, she' didn't know. She pulled Joe to his feet.

Shadows streamed through the arch into the garden. Hooves drummed and dogs howled.

She pointed ahead. "Remember the broken wall?"

"Yeah."

"Let's go." God, she hoped she hadn't become so turned around that she'd lost the right way. She grabbed his hand, and they half-ran, half-stumbled, slipping and sliding. It didn't matter how much noise they made now. Speed was more important. She put a hand around Joe's waist, half-holding him up.

The creatures had converged where the stream met the steps, closing in on her scent. In a moment, they'd be on the terrace and able to track her. Ahead, a broken shape gave her hope. In a shambling run, more jog than sprint, they made their way toward it. Something caught her hood, but she wrenched herself forwards with a yell and came free. Ahead stood the broken wall behind the cottage and she didn't look back. She didn't have time. The hunt was on and she did what prey always did.

She ran.

CHAPTER SIXTEEN

Night Secrets

JEAN'S EYES SMARTED at the sudden brightness of the lights at the Glenshane service station. The first part of the drive, following benign County Down roads and across a sleeping Belfast, had been easy. Now they'd reached the North-west, the weather had begun to show its teeth.

"Coffee," said Robert. "And get some supplies in the car. Just in case."

It was the first either of them had spoken in miles. They'd fallen into a sullen silence borne of her anger that, even now, Robert was telling her nothing, and his annoyance at what he claimed had been nagging.

She unclicked her seatbelt and went in. Amid the low hum of the refrigerator units Jean popped some energy bars into her basket and two bottles of lucozade. For health's sake, she added bananas and oatmeal biscuits. Robert fetched two coffees from the machine, and they were back in the car within ten minutes.

Snow covered the tarmac, brown where the gritters

had been out earlier that night. Slowly, the car climbed the mountain. With each mile, the snow grew deeper. Somewhere near the top, the storm came back and visibility dropped to near zero. An empty pub, claiming itself the highest in Ireland, flashed to their right and then vanished. They began to descend, engine whining as Robert held the car in high gear. As they neared the bottom of the pass the snow finally eased and visibility became a little better. In all that time, they'd passed no other vehicle.

"Right," Robert said. "You wanted to know what happened, in Donegal. I'll tell you – what I can, anyhow." The dashboard's light gave him an eerie half-blue look, more stranger than someone familiar. Jean couldn't tell if Robert felt now able to tell her because of the darkness, that it hid him, or if it was that they were running out of miles: once through Derry, they'd be across the border into Donegal.

"You remember that Belle and I were taken down to our gran's that Christmas? The year it happened?" He gave a hollow laugh. "Tonight brings that journey back – we drove up in snow that year, too. This was in the seventies, before the wonders of ABS and the car was skidding everywhere."

"I remember." Her memories of Belle were etched in her mind forever. "You wanted to go, Belle didn't."

"Want is probably an exaggeration. But I was older and knew we had to go. Gran wasn't well – she'd just had her first stroke. Belle was upset, though. She fought like a demon not to go. She was sure Santa wouldn't find us." He half-smiled. "I was pretty sure he was in the front of the car with a bootful of presents but didn't tell her. I figured she'd have worked it out in another year anyway, so why spoil her fun. I wasn't always an evil big brother, you know."

"Just sometimes," Jean said and smiled. "You used to tease us terribly." There had been no real malice in that Robert, she remembered. His pointed ability to hurt people, to find the things they were ashamed of and use them, came later.

"Anyway, we got to Gran's in one piece. You were never there, I don't think…?"

"No." The house had been sold long before she'd married Robert, but she had seen pictures. A sturdy farmhouse set in a cottage garden with a greenhouse to the side, it was a substantial property. She'd driven past the house during one of her summer visits, and had parked up just beyond the driveway. She hadn't been able to resist walking back to look at the place. Leaning on an old fence at the bottom of the garden, the house had been easily recognisable and she'd felt better about seeing it, as if she had another piece of the jigsaw in place. "But I've seen it. Big old place. Iron railings on all the windows. Formidable."

"That's right. She said iron was important, where she lived. Did you see the garden?"

"Yes." After watching for a time, she'd become sure that the occupants were out and had pushed open the front gate and walked in. The garden had stretched the whole way behind the house in a series of paths and small gardens that had formed a crazy sprawl. She could have spent all day in it, but for the small matter of not having a convenient excuse for doing so.

"Then you'll understand when I say that Gran's house was – special."

Robert spoke with a wistfulness she'd rarely heard before. Normally he was precise in his words, choosing them with care. He'd have come up with something more exact than 'special', and it would have sounded less honest for having done so.

"We'd visited before, of course, but not in the winter. She normally came to us for Christmas and we went to her in the summer and got to run riot all around the place. Except that year she was too ill and decisions needed to be taken about what to do with her, and mum and dad thought it would be easier to go up and deal with everything." He turned the wipers onto intermittent and darted Jean a quick glance. "You know Belle could be…." His lips pursed. "Sensitive…. She got hunches about things."

"I remember." It was why she'd been so quick to believe in Amelia's gift. After knowing Belle, who could tell the history of a place within moments and had an uncanny knack of seeing depths in a person that Jean never could, she had no doubt that some people were adept in ways that made no sense to those who weren't. As the years had passed, she'd become more convinced of it. Part of that was due to Robert, although she had never told him, knowing he would reject the idea. But his knack of reading people mirrored Belle's – except that where her friend had mostly found the good in a person, Robert too often found the opposite.

"Belle hated being at Gran's that winter. In the

summer, she'd always been happy, but from the moment we arrived in the snow, she complained. She wanted to go home. Had tantrums every day. You'd have thought she was five, not ten. My parents told her to stop being ridiculous. Finally, mum asked me to see if I could talk sense into her." He gave a sheepish smile. "So I cornered Belle and threatened to thump her if she didn't tell me what was going on."

She could imagine Robert doing that, and Belle threatening to thump him back. As kids they'd fought all the time.

"In the end, though, Belle didn't have to tell me." He fiddled with the lights, turning off the full beam then putting it on again, his hands fidgeting, never still. "I found out what lived in the garden all by myself. That's when that Christmas started to go to hell. Not at Glenveagh, but at my gran's house where a sensitive was staying at the wrong time of the year and attracting all the wrong attention." His mouth twisted. "And now it's December again, and it's as cold as that year, and your artist friend, who you think it sensitive, is staying in a cottage not three miles away from my Gran's garden." He put both hands on the wheel and looked straight ahead. "Now you might understand why we had to go and not waste time. Because if I'm right, she – and her partner – are in danger."

CHAPTER SEVENTEEN
The Hunt

THE BREAK IN the wall was only two feet away. Beyond it, Amelia could make out the Gardener's Cottage. She pounded towards it. Joe kept pace, his shock from being held captive broken by the adrenalin of their flight. There was no hope of escaping, she knew that. The monsters would follow them though the broken wall. But still she ran, because not to was to give up all hope.

Hoofbeats were loud behind her, and getting louder. The ground drummed. She had no idea how close the pack was and put her head down; at any moment, she expected to feel a touch on her shoulder.

She sped up as she reached the wall and clambered over. Joe boosted her, his hands on her arse pushing her forwards. She turned to help him and now she could see the hunt, only a few lengths back. The mounts' hooves sparked off the stone terrace even through the snow.

"Hurry!" She stuck out her hand and Joe took it. She pulled with all her might and he tumbled over the breached wall. Behind, the first mount drew close enough for her to see the fumes from its breath making a white cloud in the darkness.

And then it stopped, a few feet from the wall. She backed away, Joe beside her.

"You see them too?" asked Joe. "I'm not crazy, right?"

The irony of being asked that question wasn't lost on Amelia.

"I see them too." She wasn't going to comment on the crazy bit. No point of such labelling, she'd always thought. They backed away further, reaching the cottage and *still* nothing followed. A part of her wished the hunt would just get on with it and finish things; mostly she was glad of the reprieve.

They passed the cottage and reached the second wall. The walled garden lay behind it, its long grids and well-laid paths offering no hiding places. At the bottom, the castle and its long conservatory glinted in the moonlight. It provided no better for cover but at least the building was big, with towers and cellars, and had places to hide.

"We could try to get into the castle again," she said. It would be warmer, too. "We could try the conservatory this time. The glass should be more straightforward." And possibly alarmed against intruders. That cheered her. Even on Christmas night surely an alarm at this place would bring someone in.

"Better than doing nothing." Joe glanced back at the wall. "Why haven't they followed us?"

There was no sign of any of the hunt now, no way to know if they were beyond the wall, watching, or somewhere else. The darkness had swallowed them up, it seemed.

"No idea. But I don't intend to hang around and wait for them. Whatever they are."

Joe's knowledge of them unsettled her. Only her Aunt Lucy had the gift, that Amelia knew of, which meant, unsettlingly, these creatures might be more than figments of her imagination. Shaken, she crept to the gate leading into the walled garden and paused there, searching the paths, blue-grey in the moonlight. Her instincts screamed at her to be careful, to stay hidden, to not move. That wasn't an option; not when the monsters knew where they were. "Let's go."

She steered onto the garden path, keeping to the sparse shadows offered by the surrounding wall. They reached the half-way point, crossing a path that cut theirs at a right angle. That path led to an arched gap in the wall at the other side of the garden.

Movement near the entrance into the terraced garden caught her attention, her only warning before the gateway exploded with monsters. Hooves rang out. Something howled; a shape broke off from the pack, aiming for the bottom of the garden. It would cut off the castle to them.

"This way!" yelled Joe, following the right-angled path, and Amelia had no choice but to follow the only way open to them. Unhelpfully, the thought of being herded came to her.

"Through the arch. We can try to get into the castle another way," said Joe, his breathing laboured. He was favouring his side, she noticed, the one that had been gashed.

Amelia ran along the snow-iced path, arms out for balance, towards the break in the wall. She passed through it and into a formal garden. Plants surrounded her, hunched into the snow. Their thin branches reached to the sky like fingers; one caught her as she ran, snagging her coat so that she had to pull free.

Opposite, a closed gate of what looked to be heavy wood banded in black, blocked their path.

"For Christ's sake," said Joe. "Something has to be easy this night." He yelled up at the sky. "Hear me, up there! Something easy, please."

But nothing was easy, especially in this estate, where it felt as if they were moving in trapped circles. Amelia slammed against the gate. The rough wood was full of splinters and unmoving. She fumbled with its bar, but it took Joe's hand over hers to push it down.

A howl came from behind them. *Too close.* She pushed on the gate, Joe helping, and it opened onto a narrow woodland path. Amelia dived through. Joe followed and, together, they slammed the gate closed. Both leant against it, breathing heavily.

Behind the gate, a horn sounded. Amelia couldn't help feeling that the monsters were having fun, that this wasn't just a hunt but some kind of sport. Something thudded against the gate. She grabbed up a branch from the ground and hoisted it.

"What are you doing?" asked Joe.

"I'm going to hit them with my stick," she said. Joe's mouth twitched. She held the wood higher. She might look ridiculous but she continued to face the gate, mouth dry. She might wipe the smile off at least one of their faces.

"Aren't you trying to escape?" said a high-pitched voice from behind Amelia.

Amelia spun into a crouch. A little girl stood on the pathway, dressed in a red coat. She couldn't be more than ten years old. Her hair was braided into pleats that fell either side of her head, and she looked vaguely familiar. In the darkness, she seemed to be part of the woodland, made of the shadows around them.

"They like someone new to play with." The little girl's lip wobbled. "They get bored of me."

Bored of her? What did that even mean? Amelia crouched. "What are they?"

"Who the hell are you talking to?" asked Joe. "Amelia…?"

He couldn't see this child, but he could see the monsters? At a new howl, Amelia turned her attention back to the child. She'd work out what this all meant later, when there was time.

"The creatures in the garden. Do you know what they are?"

"Yes. Come with me. I know where to hide." The girl, or whatever she was, held her hand out and there was something so innocent about the gesture, so open and honest, that Amelia found herself taking it.

"Where can we go?" asked Amelia. She glanced over her shoulder at Joe. How to explain this to him? What if she was wrong, trusting the child? The whole thing was so bizarre, Amelia expected to wake up, cold, in the Gardener's Cottage, Joe asleep against her.

"I have places. But if they find us here, they'll follow." A shadow of fear crossed the child's face at a shattering bang on the gate. "That's what they do."

She was so thin and young. She looked nothing like a

monster. Amelia could not leave her alone in this forest of horror.

"Joe. Will you trust me?" She should have told him about her gift ages ago but she'd had it drummed into her, over so many years, not to tell that she hadn't brought it up.

To get him believe tonight, when they had no time, would be impossible. "I think I know where to go." Or she would, soon.

"Are you coming?" asked the child. "You need to be quick."

The gate shuddered. Another thud and the wood bowed.

Joe joined Amelia, a stick in his own hand. "Good. Get going, then. I'll hold them off."

"You will not!"

With a gun-shot-crack, the gate shattered.

"Joe," Amelia yelled. "Come with me!" She reached her hand out to him, but he didn't take it.

Monsters poured through the gate, blocking Joe from her sight. A huge dog leapt at Amelia, a mount not far behind it. On its back, one of the leathered creatures swung its blade. Amelia ducked by instinct.

"You need to come now!" shouted the child, her voice shrill with terror.

"Joe!" Amelia yelled. He didn't reply. More monsters surged through the opening.

"Come on," The girl tugged her hand, surprisingly strong for someone so young. "We have no time!"

Another hound broke away from the pack. It aimed directly for Amelia, a mounted rider in tandem behind.

The rider's eyes fixed on her. The hound leapt.

The child pulled Amelia hard enough to drag her out of the hound's reach. Amelia skidded in the snow, threatened to go down – knowing the monster would be on her before she could recover – but just kept her footing. The girl tried to pull her off the path, into the deeper forest.

"Wait! I have to get my friend!" Amelia couldn't leave a child in these woods – but she couldn't leave Joe, either. She wrenched her hand free.

"You can't. He's a man." The child spat the word, then grabbed Amelia's wrist again. She took on the shape of someone taller, and older, before the image of a young girl stabilized again. She dragged Amelia off the path, and she could do nothing to break free, so strong was the hand that held her.

CHAPTER EIGHTEEN
Glamour

THE GLENSHANE PASS lay well behind Jean and Robert. The lack of traffic brought home to Jean how crazy it was to hare off on a mercy mission that might not even be needed. They should be at home Skyping with Adrian in Australia, not traipsing over mountain passes.

"You said there was something in the garden," she said to Robert. "What was it?"

Robert stared ahead and she wondered if he would answer. His hands tightened, almost imperceptibly, on the steering wheel.

"Belle said they were monsters." A half-smiled danced on his lips. "I, on the other hand, thought they were rather magnificent."

"What were they?" *And why did Belle see them as monsters?* Jean thought of her skittish friend, who tried to see the best, not the worst. Robert had just described a mirror image of the siblings she knew.

"They were... people. They were tall, and lean – all men, no women."

"Why did you think they were magnificent?" They rounded a curve and the road's emptiness stretched ahead. No one even knew they'd taken this trip. If they didn't return, would the journey be traced from the CCTV cameras they might have passed? And why had she even thought that. Of course they would return.

"They had a way about them. So confident. And glad to see me." Robert's voice had grown warm, almost happy. "But it wasn't just the fae – the men, I mean. They had horses, too, and they were the finest I'd ever seen."

If Robert said a horse was fine, it would be. No matter how much their estate cost to upkeep, a white elephant of a place, he would never give up his stud-horses. Nor should he – whilst the keeping of them was eye-wateringly expensive, he got a good return, and that was all down to his knowledge. The ability to spot a foal with potential had repaid them many times, as had an uncanny knack of matching horses to breed.

"Huge and all black. I didn't know the breed. I still don't."

"You must."

Robert knew horses like some people knew their football team.

"No, really, I don't. I've never come across the same horses anywhere else." The happiness faded from his voice. "God knows, I've tried. All the hours I've spent talking to dealers across the country, to vets, scouring the net, and I have never seen the same breed of horse before or since."

"Did Belle like the horses?" asked Jean, steering him back to the story. "She was normally good with animals."

"Not this time." Robert rolled his eyes. "You know Belle. So skittish when she wanted to be."

So intuitive, Jean thought. Not one to be fooled.

"No," said Robert. "She hated the horses just as much as she hated the men. She got upset when I wanted to spend more time with them."

"So, who were they?" pushed Jean. "These men? They must have come from somewhere."

"I assume so, but I have no idea where," said Robert. "I first met them in Gran's garden. Right at the bottom, where the apple trees were, in a hollow where the garden dipped to the stream. They weren't visible to the house from there. In fact, I only found them by chance. There was a hare on the lawn, and I'd never seen one before, only rabbits. I wanted to get a look but it ran. I followed and there they were, waiting for me."

This was all so un-Robert-like. Running after a hare. Finding people at the bottom of the garden but never challenging them as to who they were, or why they were there. "Just like that? You fell over them?"

"Pretty much. I don't know how long they'd been there. They beckoned me over and, once I saw their horses, I couldn't walk away. Instead, I went up to them."

Hadn't he known his stranger-danger? Or did he think that was for girls, and that he was safe? Knowing the Robert of her childhood, he possibly did.

"How many were there?" And how on Earth could this all have happened unseen? His Gran's garden had been a good size, yes – but not big enough to hide a posse of men, complete with their horses.

"Oh, a good few. Some were half-hidden amongst the

trees, watering their mounts, as I recall. Others were in the trees. I assumed they were gamekeepers, at first, given the horses and their garb – dark, very practical. Maybe poachers." He grinned. "It all felt very glamorous."

"Did you tell your parents about them?"

"No. How could I? 'Hi, mother, father, there are creatures in Gran's garden.' Even if they believed me, they had enough on their plate without me giving trouble. Besides… they were my secret. Later I found out they were Belle's, too."

The car had grown warm and stuffy. Jean leant against the door, glad of its coolness.

"The leader got to his feet when I appeared," said Robert.

"How did you know he was the leader?"

"It was obvious. The way he carried himself. His height. Maybe seven feet, with hair that he had tied back with leather. He had a lean face, beard-shadowed, with a long scar on one cheek. But he was good looking. He looked the way I'd have liked to look myself." Robert touched his forehead. "I can never forget him."

"What did he say to you?" She hated the sound of this man.

"He greeted me by name and let me stroke his horse. It whinnied when I did, lowering its head as if welcoming me, and he told me I was good with horses – which I already knew, but I was pleased he had noticed. The other men were asking about who I was, and what sports I played. They were *interested* in me. You know?"

Jean caught the hitch in his voice, the unspoken words. They were interested in him at a time when his parents, distracted and worried, weren't. They were interested in Robert, who was so often overlooked as the oldest, expected to get on with things and not compete with the flighty Belle, who drew attention like a light drew moths. As her best friend, Jean remembered what it had been like to be in Belle's circle and how easy it had been to be overlooked. She had never minded – she was as in awe of Belle as everyone else – but had basked in the reflected glory of being the chosen confidante. Best Friends Forever, Belle had proclaimed her, declaring they could have no secrets, and they never had.

"So, you were flattered," she said, and could hear the disdain in her voice. "That's why you liked these men?"

Robert straightened in the driver's seat. "Well, yes. I was. And why not? They were amazing with their horses and the dark clothes. And they were fun, telling jokes and sparring with me. I wanted to stay and not have to go back to the house and all its misery. But they had to go, they said. Then they warned me to tell no one about them, and especially not my Gran."

"And they left?"

"For then. But they came back the next day. That's when they asked me to bring Belle to them. I didn't want to."

"Why not?"

"I didn't want to share them with her." He gave a small, bitter smile. "I know, I know… but I was only twelve. I'd never had so much attention. It was hard to give that up. So the leader told me we'd make a deal. He told me I could ride out on a hunt with them if I brought Belle to them."

"Did you want to?" Jean's stomach had clenched and she put her hand on it, trying to ease the tension. But Robert's talk of a hunt had brought back her winter dreams of drumming hooves and hunters' horns.

"God, yes. Ride one of those horses? I would have loved to. They were big, smart, and wilder than any stallion I'd seen. I knew I could ride one and it would be like no other."

She could see how that would have appealed to Robert. She shivered, thinking of how she'd always wondered if Belle had been lured away by the promise of a dog. Now, it seemed it had been Robert who'd been lured, not Belle.

"They told me I could join them. But first, I had to bring Belle to them. They said she'd been lonely, too, and that she should meet them. That was the deal." He stared ahead, bereft. "They told me that was all I had to do. Introduce her. What harm could it do?" He looked over at Jean, and his eyes were beseeching her to understand. "They didn't seem dangerous. There was no hint of what might happen. So, I agreed to bring Belle to meet them. Except our parents decided to take us out the next day, to get rid of what they called cabin fever. We went to Glenveagh." Jean steeled herself for what must come. "That was the day Belle died."

CHAPTER NINETEEN

The Forest

THE CHILD IGNORED Amelia's attempts to break away and get back to Joe. She held onto her wrist with a strength at odds with her size and age. It made no sense for a child to be in the forest on such a cold night with no one looking for her. But a crazy hunt led by monsters didn't make sense, either, nor banshees at a harbour.

"I have to go back," said Amelia. "Joe's…" She couldn't say what he might be. The unfamiliar ring dug into her finger, anchoring her. "I have to find him."

"You can't. The hunt will have him by now." The child's voice was hard-edged. "They'll like him a lot. And he likes *you* a lot. Which means we can't go back. We've come too deep."

The words made no sense. They could not have travelled far in such a short space of time. Yet the hunt could no longer be heard at all.

"Let me go," Amelia said. Her wrist felt like it was burning, and she tried to shake herself free from the girl. "I said, let me *go*!"

"Do you promise not to run?"

Amelia hesitated and that was enough to make the child strengthen her grip until Amelia yelled out. The pain convinced her this wasn't a dream.

"You must promise not to run!" The words were petulant, those of one used to getting her own way.

Where would she run to? Amelia had no idea where they were in the forest, and she could not risk being taken by the hunt. She'd never help Joe if she was.

"I won't run," she said. *Yet*; she thought.

The child let go of Amelia's wrist and Amelia rubbed at the reddened skin.

"I'm sorry I hurt you. But the hunt would have done worse. I had to get you away." The girl started to make her way through the trees. Her footing was sure, each step a dance through the thick woodland. She picked past branches and brambles that followed no logic and never stumbled. She looked back, and beckoned Amelia. "Come on. It's safe."

Amelia followed, a distance away, not intending to allow herself to be caught again. Where the child had walked easily, Amelia had to fight her way through. The woodland was dense, the ground underfoot hard and slippery. Amelia stepped over a half-ruined wall, into the squared-off foundation of what must have been a building. It had been small, perhaps an ice house or somewhere workers had sheltered.

The girl waited in the center, coat limp, shoulders glistening with snow. She looked tiny in the woodland, like someone lost in a storybook. Her head was bowed, and she took no notice of Amelia. She raised her arms and murmured something Amelia couldn't make out. A rhyme, perhaps. At last, the girl lifted her head. "This way. We're through the ward."

"What ward?" Was it a colloquial name for the ruins they were in?

The child stepped onto a twisting path that led through the woods. Amelia hadn't noticed her coming out of the ruins, and didn't remember doing so herself, but they were back in woodland.

This wood was different, though. It must be buried deep in the estate, away from the tourist trails, because it was wilder and older. Low brambles lined the path, hunched with light snow, and the tree trunks were thick and covered in broken bark. The air had grown still, almost watchful.

"I had to bring you here," said the child. She seemed almost apologetic. "I need Mother Beith." She angled into woodland that looked like it had never been planted or planned. Roots twisted around roots; branches entwined with branches; trunks embraced ivy trains like lovers. As she crunched through leaves, Amelia realised the snow had vanished and it was clear underfoot, with no ice to skid on.

She slowed. Her breath was sharp, exhausted from the run, but the child appeared barely winded, skipping across a shallow ditch to a copse of trees as if she were a woodland creature. Amelia stopped at the edge of the soft bank. There were no footprints.

"Where are we?" she asked. In the same estate, or another world? Lost, or found? But it was only half the question, and not the important half. "And who are you?"

The child halted on the other bank, caught in the moonlight, hands on hips, bossy and sassy, nothing like the scared girl Amelia had first encountered.

"Come on," she said. "The ward will not be strong enough to hold them for long."

"I need an answer," said Amelia. She'd had enough of this game. The child couldn't be real or she'd have frozen by now.

A howl behind Amelia made her heart quicken.

"I am taking you to Mother Beith," said the child. "She will protect us. As to who I am...." She gave a small, sad smile. "I am of the forest. It's my home. It has been for years."

Another howl, closer, followed by the sound of the horn convinced Amelia to get moving. She'd find the answers she needed later and, in the morning, she'd get this little girl out of the forest and hand her into the police. From there, surely, they would find who she belonged to.

Amelia jumped the ditch but landed short and splashed into what must be mud along its bottom. She pulled her rapidly sinking foot free, her hiking boots giving a sucking sound as they emerged, and made it to the furthest bank. She dreaded to think of the trail she must be leaving. She sensed a low drumming sound in the air; a warning of what might come.

"They're following," said the girl. "They'll find the ward soon." She darted away so quickly Amelia that had to dash after her to have any chance of keeping up. A bramble caught her cheek, reminding her this was real and not a dream. Dreams could be sharp, but they didn't leave a trail of blood through skin, blood that could be touched and tasted.

The girl stopped, just ahead, foot tapping in impatience. She waited until Amelia caught up and then wheeled away, leading the way into a glade. In its centre a circle of birch trees, their trunks shining silver in the darkness, stood. They were so silvered they appeared to give out light.

Slowly, carefully, placing each foot before moving the next, the child half-walked, half-danced to the centre of the circle. She faced the largest of the trees and bowed her head. "Mother Beith. I need your help."

The girl put her hand on the tree's trunk. "Amelia, this is Mother Beith." How had she known Amelia's name? She ran her hands over the wood. "Don't look with your eyes. Feel her."

Not sure if it was to humour the child, or because she had to know what she meant, Amelia went up to the tree. Its bark had peeled away from the trunk in places, making patterns and shapes that she traced with her hand. It took her a moment to grasp what the child meant but the shapes within the bark were familiar. She traced them carefully, finding a long limb here, a roundel of a breast there, the bowed line of a pair of lips, smooth enough they felt like a kiss under Amelia's palm.

She looked up, knowing what she must find and, yes, there in the shining bark she could just make out the pattern of a face, mournful eyes dimpled in two knots.

"Oh!" Amelia dropped her hands from the trunk and stumbled back. "What is it?"

"Who, not what. This is Mother Beith. She'll help us. I hope."

"The tree will?"

The child nodded, solemnly.

"Well, that's good. I think." Amelia picked out the tree's features again. God knew, they needed help. Not just her and the girl but Joe, too. Bile rose, driven by the fear that the hunt were chasing her again because their business with him was done, that he lay, crushed and wounded – *worse* – where the hunt had discarded him.

She doubled over, sure she would vomit but only bile came up, bitter and thin. She could have snatched him, or refused to leave. She could have fought the monsters alongside him and allowed the child to escape. She had done none of those things. She had hesitated, doubting herself, giving the child the chance to take her from him.

Joe would never have left the gate. He'd have stood and fought, no matter what, and he'd have given a good account of himself to the monsters. Whereas she had run, like a coward.

A branch moved under her hand, as if giving comfort. Its warmth surprised Amelia. The wood throbbed in a pulse that resembled a heartbeat.

"Can you help him?" she asked, but there was no response. "Can you help Joe?" She turned to the child. "What is this tree?"

"Mother Beith. A Skeagh-shee. A tree spirit."

There were no such things. But monsters didn't exist, either, or mounts that weren't horses. Or banshees. And at least this imaginary creature wasn't trying to kill her, or anyone else, just yet.

"Will she help?"

"Maybe." The child laid her hand on the tree,

caressing the bark. Lines were etched into it, Amelia saw, a distinct pattern of slashes that meant nothing to her.

"This Lady needs to claim protection," the child said. She sounded older, her voice more rounded and polite. The half-hinted at shape from earlier, the willowy lady, returned, edging the child's form. "She will harm no branch and hurt no seed. The hunt seeks her, and she must be spared." She hugged the tree, small hands clutching the splitting bark, her cheek turned against the wood. "Please. She's important." Her eyes glistened. "To me. She's important to me."

The tree seemed to stare at Amelia. She didn't know what to say to prove herself worthy – or if there was anything that *could* be said. She'd left Joe. Her cowardice must shine from her; her unworthiness.

A branch lowered to the ground. The child climbed onto it.

"Come on," she said. "The hunt will be searching. They'll reach the grove soon."

"What about Joe?" asked Amelia. She wasn't going any further without some kind of assurance. If she let the tree take her, how did she even know she'd get back? "Can he be helped?"

The child leaned into the tree and whispered something. The tree responded, branches rustling, touching the next tree, which bent and touched the next in an expanding circle.

"The Mother will call to Father Daire. She can do no more."

The sound of drumming reached Amelia, ebbing and flowing, but definitely closer.

"Please! Father Daire will do what he can. You must trust!" said the girl. "I can do no more! We must stay hidden."

Getting taken herself would not help Joe. Being found in this grove, where she could be run down, would not deliver vengeance. Amelia climbed onto the branch, balancing with both hands as it dipped under her weight. It straightened and lifted, jerking so that she was thrust against the trunk, the girl tucked against her. A voice whispered to her, a breathy voice formed of wind and strength. "Do not harm our child, or we will harm you as the hunt could never do."

The tree wrapped them in its branches and lifted them into its heights. Warmth built around Amelia, warmer than the cottage had been, a proper warmth that made her fingers tingle. She curled against the trunk, her arm around the child to give balance.

Together, they waited as the hunting horns drew closer, and Amelia still knew nothing about who this child was, or what she wanted.

CHAPTER TWENTY
Finbeara

"GRAN BEGGED MY parents not to go to the estate that day," said Robert. "When my father ignored her protests, she tried my mother. They argued about it. Mum wasn't sure we should go. He said his day wasn't going to be governed by superstitious nonsense. As ever, he won."

"How do you know?" asked Jean.

Robert had been twelve at the time and his parents would not have shared such matters with him. They'd been typical big-house parents, of the 'children should be seen and not heard' variety. She'd never liked them.

"You listened!" Robert was many things – controlling to the point of obsession, rude when his patience was stretched thin – but he'd never been a sneak. "What? At the door?"

"I was told to," he said. "*He* told me to."

"Who?" But she knew who it had to be.

"The leader of the hunt," he said. "Finbeara, he calls himself."

Chill gripped Jean's heart at the slip of the tongue. Calls, not called.

"He came to me, the morning we left for Glenveagh. He said there would be obstacles in our way, that the women of the house would give battle to him. His face twisted when he spoke of my Gran. That was one thing I didn't like about him."

"So why did you listen? If you didn't like him."

The car slowed a little. Robert had taken his foot off the accelerator. She wondered if he'd forgotten where he was, lost in memories, but he sped up a moment later.

"Oh, I liked him. But sometimes he had an edge I was uncomfortable with." He gave a harsh laugh. "But – he played me so well. He said it was how a person was to be found worthy; face challenges and overcome them. He even did an initiation with me, as if I was joining some kind of exclusive club."

"What did you have to do?" She was agog, half-dreading what it might have been, half-excited.

"Nothing difficult. He gave me a vampire-mark, he called it, on my neck by brushing his teeth on it." He tilted its head. "You've seen it. I told you it was a birthmark." He lifted his head, turning it to the dash light so that she could see the mark on the slender turn of his neck. "And then he took a blade that he carried at his waist. It was sharper than any I've ever seen, like a razor. He slit my arm with it, and bloodied me. He said I had one other thing to do to be worthy and that was to bring Belle to Glenveagh. He'd already asked me to bring her to the garden, but I'd failed. This was my second chance."

"So Belle hadn't already met him?"

"Not at gran's. I asked Belle to come to the orchard and she refused. She said she knew what I wanted and she wasn't going. She told me they were monsters – Finbeara, and his crew. We argued about it, and I handled it badly and she wouldn't come."

"How did you handle it?" Had he hit Belle? Robert had been very capable of doing so; Belle and him had spent half their childhood bashing each other.

"I told her a lie. I told her I'd found a hare – which I had, remember – and that I wanted her to see it. But, you know Belle. She always knew a lie. She told me she knew what was in the orchard. She asked me if I'd seen my new friends' real faces. She told me their horses were the corpses of stolen horses, not anything alive. She warned me to stay away from them. Then she locked herself in her room." He half-smiled. "The full works. Chair under the handle, key removed from the door. She only came out when our parents called her down the stairs."

"Did you tell Finbeara that she was scared?"

His face was strained. Robert, who always looked younger than he was and took trouble to do so, now looked his full fifty-and-then-some-years.

"No." He swallowed. "I didn't want to go, knowing he wanted to meet Belle. But I thought of the horses, and how I'd been welcomed, and so I didn't speak up and Dad had his way." His hands clenched on the steering wheel. "Not that my objection would probably have made a difference. But I've always wondered if it might." He wiped his mouth. "Christ. This is hard. I've never told anyone this, Jean."

Had shame stopped him? Or fear? Both could be

strong emotions. Perhaps he'd been scared what his story might do to his parents. Bad enough to have to live with what happened to Belle; for his parents to believe Robert was lying, or touched, would have been another layer of hurt.

"Maybe it will be good to face what happened," she said.

"Maybe. God knows silence hasn't stopped Finbeara eating away at me."

"And you did it – you brought Belle to Glenveagh?"

"I did," he confirmed. "My gran told my father it was dangerous to take a child like Belle to the estate. He ignored her. He'd been brought up in that house with its iron-clad doors, but he'd never believed any of the Fae stuff. It took a special kind of pig headedness to achieve that, but you know my father. My mother wavered. She knew Belle was special, even if she never said it. You can't carry a child like Belle and bring her up without knowing she was – different." He licked his lips. "God. I can feel how scared I was that she'd lock herself back in the room and not go. I didn't know what I'd tell Finbeara." His face was raw with pain. "I told her I'd take care of her, that we'd stick together and convinced Belle it would be all right, knowing I was lying. Knowing that I didn't care what happened to her, so long as Finbeara was pleased. I let my parents take me and Belle to Glenveagh, despite my gran's protests, knowing what I was doing was wrong. My gran knew more about the spirits than I did. So did Belle. I should have listened, but I didn't." A grim smile touched his lips. "Which means, in a way, you've always been right, Jean. I didn't kill Belle. But I did bring her to her death."

CHAPTER TWENTY-ONE

The Grove

THE DRUMMING CHANGED from low and ominous to something sharper that reached through the tree's trunk to Amelia's bones. With the drumming came the barking of hounds to create a chaos of excitement, especially when the high yells of the monsters joined in.

Amelia curled her free hand around the trunk, until the wood cut into her skin, and hugged the child to her with the other arm. Whatever she was, spirit or a lost child in the forest, she deserved comfort. The branch underneath shook in time with the hunt's approach.

The child's face grew pinched. Against Amelia, she was thin, birdlike and shivering. Her face was curled into Amelia's arm, hidden, her chin sharp against Amelia's skin. The equanimity she had shown in the flight through the forest was gone.

"They're powerful," she said. "They'll find us."

"Come out, come out, come out." A growled demand, made in time with the beating drums, bellowed across the forest. As previously in the terraced garden, the monster sounded amused, as if the hunt was a game.

"Easy, Mother Beith." The girl untucked herself enough to rub the trunk. Leaves rustled but the wood remained hard and unmoving under Amelia's hands, denying any comfort she offered. "They have not found this ward before."

"What's a ward?" Amelia asked, her voice low. She should not be helpless, yet she was. Defended by a child and a tree spirit when, really, she needed to understand how the girl had been able to lose the hunt. She needed to know how the garden and woods worked. She especially needed to understand the wards the girl had used to safeguard them.

"The wards are places where the worlds thin," said the girl.

"Worlds? But there's only one?"

"You know that is not so."

The certainty in the child's words silenced Amelia. Did she? She knew there were things she had seen, and felt, that did not belong in the normal world. But to go as far as to say they were from *another* world – that was superstition and nothing more. Yet Mother Beith had spoken with her, and this flimsy child survived alone in a winter forest.

"The wards offer protection to the person who opened them but they aren't always strong enough to hold back the hunt. They have the old magic, too." The girl stroked the trunk of the tree. "Some wards are stronger than others. Mother Beith's is strong, for instance, but the ruins we entered through were not. Its magic was stolen years ago, when its people were killed." She screwed up her face.

"The longer the hunt goes on, the fewer wards exist that have not been found. Once the hunt has opened a ward, they can revisit it."

The pictures on the cottage wall of had spoken of death in the estate. One harsh winter people had been expelled – during the famine, of all times – and left to starve. Amelia shivered, despite the tree's protection keeping the cold air from her. Had that cruelty left the estate open to these monsters, by leaving buildings ruined and empty?

"The hunt is as magical as I, or Mother Beith." The girl gave a sly glance at Amelia. "Or you. You opened a ward tonight. A powerful one, one they could not go near. I felt it."

Amelia wanted to say she wasn't magical, but that had too many strands of untruth. The denial might have worked in the past, when she was in the world of cars and people, and jobs and mortgages. But, here, deep in these ancient woods, it would be useless. She drew a deep breath, rejecting years of obeying her mother and aunt. Whether it would destroy her life as they had claimed was immaterial: she might not survive this night if she didn't learn what was needed.

"What did I open?" And how could she have when she'd never heard of a ward before. "Where?"

"I don't know. But it rang out across the forest. It would have felt old, I think. Something enclosed within walls."

Amelia's eyes widened. *An old smell, rushing at her.* A square within a square, walled in a square, encircled by walls, by the gardens and the forest itself.

"The fireplace," she said. "In the cottage?"

"A strong place," agreed the child. "Sealed before I came to the estate. Once you opened it you were safe in the cottage." Her eyes narrowed. "Why did you leave?"

"Joe… he didn't come back. I was worried." Plus, she hadn't known it was safety the fireplace offered; it had felt dangerous to her. Just as the child did, and Mother Beith. Perhaps danger sat beside protection in this place; perhaps they were a side to each other.

"The hunt drew you out."

"Yes." Using Joe as a lure to bring her into the terraced garden. They were clever, these monsters. She swallowed and her throat was dry, almost rasping. "So the hunt know where we are?"

"Probably. The old ruin is a weak device," said the child. "But it was the only one I could reach in time, to take me into this wood and the stronger wards. It's not well hidden from sight, or blessed by the wood spirits." She shrugged. "If they have tracked us to that ward, they will come through. And, once through, they will sense Mother Beith's circle. They will know where we have come to."

The drumming became a crashing. Soon, surely, it would explode into the grove.

The child clutched Amelia's arm, her grip the same iron-hard as earlier.

"This is important. You must understand. The wards allow you to cross into the other-world. When you open one, you command it until another being has the power to breach it. The hunt has plenty of power. And tonight it will have more."

"Why?" Her heart beat in her chest, the slow beat of fear.

"The moon."

Not by hurting Joe, but by the moon. Amelia swayed, dizzy, and had to clutch the branch beneath her.

"The hunt come only during the deep winter moons. Tonight the waxing gibbons is upon the moon, and they will be strong." The child swallowed, scanning the ground. "Once they find the first ward –"

"And you're sure they will?"

"Of course. It was not well hidden. I told you that." She sounded petulant. "Our best hope is they take their time finding their way through Mother Beith's ward; that morning comes before they do." Her eyelids shivered, as if with a tic, as she looked down and away. "That they are distracted."

It had to be asked.

"And what about Joe?" Amelia said, her words thick. "Do the wards keep him safe?"

Before an answer came, a hound exploded into the glade, sending up a long howl. More followed, appearing between each tree. The trees bunched together, branches touching branches, leaves twisting with leaves. Only Mother Beith remained where she was, tall and proud.

One of the monsters ducked between two trees. On its head, it wore antlers, bleach-white and pointing to the sky. It paused, reached up, and contemptuously broke a twig off the nearest tree. Mother Beith trembled.

The monster stepped into the centre of the glade. Amelia's dangling legs tensed. She wished she'd drawn them up. She let go of the branch below and pulled the child against her. She felt as insubstantial as air.

The monster stood at least seven feet tall. Its arms and legs were corded with muscles, its chest honed and defined, all hardness and sinew. It was, from its shape, more human – and definitely man, there were no soft breasts that might denote a female – than animal, but a misshapen man, moulded from something foul.

It stopped and relaxed, stance open, not trying to hide. Once again, the sense that the bastard was enjoying itself came to Amelia. Its mouth twisted and on its teeth she could see dark marks that could be blood and thought of Joe.

A smell reached her, of stagnant ponds untouched by lightness, holding dead things at their core. Images flickered through her mind, so quick she could barely hold them. The last, of a bare rose tree pointing its branched fingers at the sky, made her bite down to stifle her shock. That had been her image and now it was stolen.

"Hello, tree-bitch. Where is my prey?" The creature stalked towards Mother Beith. Its legs were hoofed, leaving a distinctive trail in the grass and at last, for sure, Amelia knew what had been in the garden at the cottage. Had they been, even then, preparing to hunt? They could go anywhere, those hooves, up any cliff. Perhaps even up a tree. "Have you seen my prey? I want to find her. And keep her."

The child stiffened. Amelia's chest hitched, threatening to spill into a howl. She could hardly bear facing the hunt tonight – what of this child, who had faced it before, many times?

"Begone." The wind sighed around Amelia, vibrating

in her fingers, rumbling through the branch she was sitting on. "This glade belongs to me. *My* ward will not be breached."

The branches came around Amelia and the child, a circle of protection.

The monster gave a low growl. What had once, perhaps, been fingers curved into claws. With a snarl it leapt at the tree, digging into the bark and raking the wood. Mother Beith gave a high whistle that could not have been any wind. It twisted, branches whipping futilely at the monster, who dodged easily from each blow. Amelia tightened her grip, sure she would fall.

"Begone, monster!" A thick branch swept the beast to the side, sending the beast tumbling across the glade. It growled and came onto its haunches. The branches of other trees swung to block its path. "You have no place here!"

More monsters fought their way past the guarding trees, their claws digging into soft bark, their hunting blades – long, thin, and deadly sharp – slicing twigs and branches. They attacked from all sides, stabbing the trees, pulling their bark in long strips. The hounds' muzzles closed on brittle wood. Branches whipped from side to side with a noise that sounded like crying. Cold air flooded around Amelia, ripping away the false warmth. The circle of branches around her grew ragged.

"There!" The leader leapt for her, claws outstretched. The child kicked down at it, her aim sure, and it staggered back. It grinned up. "Two! We have two!"

Amelia got to her feet in a smooth movement she'd never have guessed she was capable of, but had nowhere to go. She balanced on the wide branch. The clearing below was filled with the creatures.

"What do we do?" she yelled, but the child was dumbcast, wide-eyed and staring. Amelia didn't think she'd ever seen so much terror on a face. "What happens next?"

The child got to her feet, chin raised, eyes fixed. "You were so nearly free." Her hand trembled on the trunk. The tree shuddered and shook. "My name is Belle. Remember me."

She stepped off the branch, into thin air. For a moment she hung, denying gravity.

"No!" Amelia tried to grab her coat but, like grabbing a thistle-clock, it slipped from her grasp.

The child fell into the pack. They launched themselves at her. Her cries were lost in their snarls. Amelia's hands were slick with sweat, her legs trembling so much they barely held her. She had never known fear like this but she jumped. She would not leave the child to face the hunt alone.

A horn blared. The lead-monster pulled back, ready to attack with bloodied claws. The horn sounded again and the pack turned on tail and left the grove.

Amelia dropped to the now-empty forest floor. Belle was gone. When Amelia lifted her hand, a red mark showed on her wrist, the only sign that she had run through a forest last night, evading a hunt.

And then it came to her, who the child was and where she had seen her picture. Belle, from Templeton House. The child in the sepia picture, lost in time. She stood in the silent grove and knew that she'd seen a ghost.

CHAPTER TWENTY-TWO

Fae

THE ROAD OUT of Derry into was carpeted in white and cut through with the brown scurf of slush. No lights shone from any house they passed: the power must still be off across a wide area of the county. As they left the city, the roads grew worse again.

"So, you went to the estate?" she asked, determined to make Robert tell her everything that had happened, without wriggling off the hook as he no doubt wanted. "The whole family, despite what your gran said."

"We did. I was glad to get away from Gran, actually, at that point." Robert tapped the steering wheel. "I loved her, of course, but never understood her. But I admired her, that day. If she had been a bit stronger – she was still recovering from the stroke – she might have stopped us going. As it was, my parents decided she'd gotten herself upset and would benefit from a quiet day." He swallowed. "All the time, I worried she would convince my parents not to go."

"Were you scared?" It seemed like he still was,

although he'd only mentioned excitement.

"Yes." The admission has no hesitation, a thing so un-Robert-like, it frightened her, too. What had she done, sending Amelia to that estate?

"Of Finbeara? Or something else?" she asked.

"Him, yes, for sure." His voice was husky and she knew she was touching the centre of something he'd never wanted to share. Shame, perhaps, or the fear of seeming weak. "I'd taken the knee and knew that if I failed him, he'd treat me as one of his men. That he would show me no mercy for failing."

"You'd seen him be bad to his men?"

"No!" A pause. "But I saw how they were with him. How, when he raised his voice, they winced away from him. I saw the scars on their skin. One of them, his back was criss-crossed with them. He never covered them up and, once, when he was slow in currying the horses, Finbeara asked if he wanted more to display. That man, he was the lowest. He did all the harder jobs with the horses, he ate after the others, he even deferred to me. I didn't want to be that man. I wanted to be someone that mattered."

"You still wanted to carry out Finbeara's commands, even knowing all that."

Robert laughed, and it had no humour. "I didn't *want* to, Jean. I had to." He lifted one hand from the wheel and squeezed it into a fist. "He had me like this. Like he could squeeze me dry, if he wanted to. I was nothing more than his toy."

"Did your gran know any of this?" Jean didn't believe that she had. She remembered the old woman with her harsh brogue and the big boots and shawls she'd worn, doubling them up as hoods or blankets, so that half the time she was hidden and the other half looking out sharply. She had doted on Belle and ignored everyone else. Not just Jean, of course, dismissed as the plain friend from the village, but Robert too. If she had known there were monsters in the garden who threatened Belle, she would have found a way to stop them.

"No. Apparently the fence around the garden – iron, the whole way around – had been breached in the summer, when she had first taken ill. She hadn't known about it – she was rarely in the garden that year."

"Finbeara breached it?"

"No. He couldn't. But … I am not the only person he drew into his world. There have been others who do his bidding. One of them could easily have broken the iron ring. If she had known, she'd have never let me stay. She'd have known I could become ensnared with Finbeara. By then I was as ensnared as I could be. Ensnared enough to get into that car, tell Belle to shut up, and let my parents drive us into Glenveagh."

"What happened when you got there?" She had never expected anything like this. She'd always been sure, somewhere deep in her heart, that Belle had been hurt by someone in the family. The way Robert's parents had shushed the authorities up – she was sure money had crossed hands – and repelled any questions afterwards had convinced her. Now, it seemed she was wrong and they'd known no more than she had. For a moment, she felt sympathy for them and then remembered how horrid they had been to her, insinuating she was a money grabber who had moved from Belle to Robert to stay in with the Big House's family.

"Belle didn't stop moaning the whole way," said Robert. "Not wanting to go, not feeling right, the crap Gran had fed her."

"Like?"

He grimaced. "The fae. She was talking about the fae. With a few ghosts and random spirits thrown in for good luck. And monsters, she said. They came into it, too."

"And that didn't make you wonder…?" This was so unlike her husband. He was smart, usually, and he had been as a child, too. "About Finbeara and his men?"

"Not then," he snapped. "I did later. When it was too late." He sighed. "Jean, don't you see it? He glamoured me." He hit the button to bring his window down and the cold fresh air whistled in. "What I saw wasn't what he really was."

"So Belle was right." She said it with no satisfaction; whatever she had expected from Robert it hadn't been this tale of defeat. "There *were* monsters."

"No. Well, in some ways but not all. Belle saw what Finbeara wanted her to see, just as much as I did." The dash light highlighted a light sheen of sweat on Robert's forehead. "That's what the fae do, and *him* more than any of them. He is whatever a person wants him to be – except when he decides to show his real self. He's clever, and subtle. The one I told you, the man he had whipped?"

"Yes."

"He wanted to be treated like that." Robert bashed one heel of his hand off the wheel of the car. "If he'd been real, not fae, he'd have still wanted to be treated like that. He wanted to be controlled and that's what Finbeara gave him." His voice hitched. "Imagine that. Being controlled by someone who knows you better than you do yourself. I wanted to feel important – so Finbeara gave me that. I wanted to be seen as above Belle, and he made me believe that, too."

"But why do people stay with him? Once they know what he's like?"

Did Jean really believe what Robert was telling her? That there could be men who weren't men but monsters? That a creature could use magic to cloud a mind? She'd sent a psychic to pick up Belle's tail, so she must believe some of this was possible. And she'd known Belle, who had been magical. Who returned in dreams, as alive as the day Jean had last seen her, aged from a girl into a willowy woman with hard eyes and a tight-lipped mouth. A woman who'd told her to send Amelia.

Yes, Jean believed.

"They stay for the hunt," said Robert. "He glamours them and then, after he has them, he turns them into his hunters and twists them. By then, they want to stay. Just like I did. Those who break free die, hunted down by the others. Once Finbeara owns you, there is only the hunt or death."

And yet Robert was here, not with the hunt, and alive. A cold knot formed in her stomach.

"Why did he want Belle at Glenveagh?" she asked. "What was the deal?"

"You'll never forgive me."

She feared he might be right. "Tell me."

A long silence. Robert's throat rippled but, at last, he

spoke: “She was to be their prey on the last night of the Hunt that year. A magical prey, the best of them all. In return, I’d be a captain.”

“You knew this and you brought Belle to him.”

“Yes. He had me under his control.” His eyes flicked to her. “You hate me.”

She did, but it was more than that. For him, it would be worse.

She pitied him.

CHAPTER TWENTY-THREE

In the Cold Morning Light

AMELIA BROUGHT HER head up, shaking off her shock. The air in the grove felt too thin, as if the grove itself was insubstantial. A wave of dizziness washed over her again, making her reach for a tree to steady herself, but this time the spell passed, leaving only nausea in its trail.

There were no monsters, no Belle, no tree spirit communicating with her. Dawn had started to break, turning the sky to a soft grey. Amelia turned in a slow circle, taking care not to miss anything, but there was nothing to see in the empty grove. She could be in any forest anywhere.

Seeking confirmation of her sanity, Amelia put her hand on Mother Beith's trunk. It was hard and cold, and there were marks of age across the bark in gnarled whorls and hacks, but she couldn't see any sense of the shape of a person within the tree, no knots that could be hands or eyes staring down at her. Beautiful though it was, it was a birch tree and nothing more.

She felt all over, seeking for any new marks on the

trunk with fumbling fingers. She shivered in the cold air, but didn't care. There must be marks left by the beasts' attack. It had been so vicious, it must have left scars. She felt all around but any marks were old. She began to believe she *had* been mistaken, that what she had seen had not been real. The way she had convinced herself that Ballygally had been a sea squall and not someone sinister. Or that the lady in the harbour had been a confused boat lady, not some harbinger of death. This time, might she have had wandered off in the night, in the cold, and become confused?

Yes, and somehow found a sheltered dell where no snow had fallen. And survived a night in the open and not have hypothermia.

Her hand touched a smooth patch on the back of the trunk. She circled the tree to where the bark was stripped back to the wood beneath, leaving a wide, broken scar. It looked like a wound.

A branch cracked under her foot, its broken end dry and undarkened by the ground's wetness. It had fallen recently. She crouched and there were more branches, all around the grove, reminding her of swords and daggers more than anything organic. The other trees had fresh slashes in their bark. She remembered swords cutting the wood, the breaking open of the trees as they tried to stop the horde from passing into the grove, how branches had whipped and snapped with a rawness of fear.

Her mouth went dry. There *had* been a hunt through the forest. Belle, the ghost-child from Jean Sweeney's painting – nothing else made sense – had been with her in the wood.

She hurried to the edge of the grove, seeking to retrace her steps, but there was no clear path through the undergrowth and nothing to tell her which way to go. She closed her eyes, concentrating. The child had led her through a wild forest, not manicured at all, to this grove. They'd passed a wall, and came through to somewhere where the snow didn't fall. A different place. One that wasn't even of the real world, Belle had said, one reached only by Belle's own magic.

Amelia bit her lips against rising panic. She hadn't understood what Belle had told about the magic of the estate, of the wards and the circles. If she tried to get out, she might end up further in. But she could not stay in this place, frozen in this fear.

She ducked out of the grove, stepping between two trees. Even if Mother Beith had been diminished – Amelia doubted anyone else's magic could work there.

In the forest, the soft ground was scuffed by hoof prints and excitement rose in her, making the ground swim. The hunt had found its way into the ward; its trail could lead her out. Quickly, she followed the disturbed ground and it wasn't hard – the horde hadn't made any attempt to hide themselves. The arrogance of that: they'd presumed their trail didn't matter, that she'd have been caught.

Amelia darted along. She must be drawing close to the estate: it felt like she'd walked longer than the previous night.

"Joe!" she called, fearing that, wherever she was, he could not hear her. And yet, she hoped for an answer. Something to give her hope. But the cold breeze returned nothing.

Belle had talked about circles of power. The grove had been one: Mother Beith and her trees in its centre, a circle within a circle. Amelia hastened through the woods, trying to make sure she went in a straight line but there was no way to be sure. She tripped on a tree stump and stumbled, hands outstretched to stop her fall but landed hard, the breath leaving her.

In front of her, just visible through brambles, she could see a low, rubbled wall. It looked like the interior of a building, plaster falling from brick.

Wards within wards. Walls within walls. A wall within a forest, within an estate, within the mountains.

She crawled to the wall and faced it, then slowly got to her feet. If she stepped over the wall, would she go deeper in? Or would she go back? Her hands tingled. Her heart was thumping, adrenalin coursing, but this was more than that, a power in her wanting to be free.

What had Belle said? That they both had magic: that was why she'd been able to pass through. She closed her eyes, thinking about where she wanted to go. The forest by the gate to the rose garden, where she had lost Joe. She imagined what had encircled it: the garden wall on one side, a ridge on another, the castle below, but didn't know what might close the fourth part of the circle.

Belle had acted without hesitation by knowing she wanted the grove. Amelia had to do the same. Belle claimed she had opened a ward when she'd opened the fireplace. She'd managed that by force, prising at the hardwood board. She didn't think that would work here, where there was no obvious join.

Okay, then. She closed her eyes. The smell of loam came all around her, a deep forest-smell. Below it, in the crisp cold air, she caught the sweetness of water nearby, making her throat moisten. She forced herself to concentrate on the forest sounds. She tried to move from this place but when she opened her eyes the ground was still clear of snow and the muddy hoof-prints still at her feet.

"Do I mutter a spell?" she said. "Don't suppose anyone could give a hint?" But the trees stayed silent. "Okay then. Abracadabra. There. I've said the magic word."

She tried again, letting her mind relax. An old smell rose; a familiar mustiness. Rustling noises came, papers turning in a breeze, and a bright light beyond her closed eyes. A cold light.

The rustling grew alongside the touch of a breeze on her cheek that hadn't been there since she'd crossed into the grove the night before. She faced the breeze, turning until it was full on her face and, when she opened her eyes, she was back at the Gardener's Cottage.

It was unchanged from the previous night: the papers were still in the neat pile she'd left them, rustling in the breeze; pieces of wood remained, piled for a kindling fire. She'd done it; found her way back, even if she still didn't know how.

She ran to the splintered door. It hadn't been forced open, or broken further; the hunt had never come into this building. They knew it was hers.

Breath hitching, she skidded down the path, taking the last section with a long turn, arms out for balance. Ahead, the gate to the rose garden waited, where she'd lost Joe.

She stopped, lungs burning, too scared to go on. This moment was the last one where everything was possible. If she went through that gate and Joe was dead… She put her hands on her stomach and tried to take a deep breath. *Courage, dear heart. Like Lucy in Narnia.* She drew a proper breath. She held the finger with the ring softly in her other hand. If she kept the ring safe, perhaps that was the charm?

"*Joe*?" Her shout seemed especially loud in the still forest. A bird took off from a tree, cawing, and her heart gave a tremor. One of the watchers? Or just a bird?

"Amelia…?" The answering call came from her left. Dizzy, she picked her way towards Joe's voice, stopping every so often to call again. The answering calls grew closer.

Something rustled to the side, and Joe stepped onto the path. His hair hung loose, pulled out of its ponytail. One arm of his coat was ripped into a long gash. But he smiled, exhausted though it seemed.

"You're okay." She touched his cheek, feeling the rasp of stubble under her hand. His skin was cold, not warm as she was used to it, but that didn't matter. He was alive. "I thought…"

"I did, too."

Amelia stumbled forwards, and Joe wrapped his arms around her, hugging her against his chest. He smelled of the familiar patchouli oil and leather, masking the slight hint of cigarettes. He smelt like Joe. She closed her eyes and allowed herself, for a moment, to take strength from his familiarity, to enjoy the sensation of being held.

An unfamiliar smell made her pull back. His oil, but

with a musty undertone. Almost sour. Something had grazed the side of his throat and a thin line of blood had trickled down in a ribbon, so much from such a small cut.

"How did you escape?" she asked. "How did you survive the night?"

He brushed her hair back and held her face in both hands, his eyes raking her, almost hungrily. She wanted to run from him and couldn't have said why, just that there was something in his look that was too intent.

"God. I barely know what was real last night, and what wasn't," he said. "There were gardens, and monsters. Some sort of hunt. It felt like a dream."

"It wasn't a dream."

"I noticed." He indicated where his jeans were gashed, the rend edged with dark blood. "I stood my ground, at the gate. I was sure the hunt would take me but thought I might slow them down at least. Give you a chance to get away."

He had stood up to them, and she had run. Amelia's throat filled with a hard lump, making it difficult to swallow. Sometime, she'd have to admit it to him.

"They ignored me! The lead one, as he passed, promised to come back." Joe paled further. "He knew my name. He said it: 'Joe McMurtry, I'll be back'. He scared the shit out of me, but…" He shook his head. "I didn't leave. I waited for him. Why would I do that?"

Why indeed? "*Did* they come back?"

He looked away. For a moment, she was sure he wouldn't answer. Fear slammed into her, the sureness that something was wrong, but when he returned his gaze to her, his face was clear.

"I don't remember them doing so. Next thing I knew it was morning and I came to, propped against the trunk of an oak tree in the middle of a thicket. I wasn't even cold. I guess I must have crawled to it for shelter. I went looking for you, and heard you calling me." He rubbed his head. "Maybe I knocked myself out when I fell. Or got concussed. I really don't remember."

Or got taken in by a tree-God.

"But you're okay?" she asked, cursing her overactive imagination. He'd spent the night in the forest. Of course he smelled of it.

"I am. And you are. We are lucky, lucky people." He rubbed his arms. "And I, for one, am cold. Let's get something warm into us and make a plan of action." He shuddered. "I don't fancy another night here. Do you?"

The thought chilled Amelia. What had Belle said?: *It's what they do.* Night after night. To a child.

They passed through the rose garden. All sense of danger had gone. The branches were just branches, not fingers. The beds were covered in soft whiteness, picture-postcard-like. Even when Amelia walked into the walled garden, which had been so full of danger the previous night, it was a vegetable garden and nothing more. The only hint of anything amiss were the now-familiar mess of hoof and paw prints in the snow.

The cottage itself gave no hint of being in any way magical. Joe went into the small kitchen to boil the kettle. Amelia stopped at the fireplace. The dark smell of the previous night had gone, only a residual mustiness left behind, not unlike the smell that had attached to Joe. The smell of the estate, she supposed. And the fireplace?

Nothing marked it as magical. There were no runes around it, or inscriptions in the brickwork. It looked and felt like nothing other than it was; a boarded-up fireplace that had been left to moulder for years. A fireplace that had got her back to safety that morning.

"Tea!" yelled Joe. Amelia joined him in the steam-filled kitchen. She took a cup, holding it with both hands, and only then realised how cold she was.

"Your turn," said Joe. His eyes were sharp over his mug. "What happened to you? How did you escape?"

Now was the time to come clean about Belle and all the things she'd seen. To tell him about her talent, and what she could do. Here, today, while it was raw and before she could put a gloss over it and lie to herself again.

The words faded on her lips, and she couldn't have said why. Perhaps it was the proximity of the garden, and the fear of what might be watching from it. Or the slight narrowing of Joe's eyes that just seemed a little too keen. Or the smell that she noticed again, stronger than earlier, that hung around him and didn't shift. But, really, it was none of those things.

She was scared he wouldn't believe her. Or, worse, that he did believe her and rejected her for it, exactly as her mother and aunt had assured her would happen if she told. That no one would want to be with someone who went off on such flights of fancy.

But this was *Joe*. She trusted him. She'd agreed to marry him. But she still couldn't tell him the truth.

CHAPTER TWENTY-FOUR
The Lido

THE SUN ROSE over the Donegal Mountains, making the morning appear benign, but slate-blue clouds threatened yet more snow. Jean shifted, trying to get comfortable, but it made no difference; her butt felt like it had been welded onto the seat. That's what 9 hours in a car would do, for a journey that should have taken a third of the time, so bad had the snow been.

"The road's a bit better here," said Jean, as they passed through Letterkenny. "Gritters have been out."

"Do you want me to go on?" asked Robert. He'd pleaded silence an hour ago, when the roads had become lethal. Following the line of Lough Swilly had been the worst part of the drive: whilst bad in Derry, it felt like Donegal had half the skies dumped on in. Twice, they'd had to get out and shovel snow to get through. Soon, once through Letterkenny, they'd be entering the hills and she thought they must be mad, but neither of them had suggested stopping. "Or have you heard enough?"

"No. Keep going." She wasn't letting him off the hook.

Before now, Belle's death had been abstract, something that had defined Jean's life into Before-Belle and After-Belle, but had never been concrete in her mind. She knew she would not have married Robert but for Belle's death and her need to get close to the family to find out what had happened in an effort to drive away her dreams. She often thought that another Jean existed in a different world, who had married the person she was supposed to and was happy. Perhaps, once she knew the truth, she'd find a way to become that person.

"We reached the estate without incident," said Robert. "We knew it well, of course. We visited most summers, but I had no idea how cold it would be to walk along the lough, or how icy the paths would be after some earlier sleet. My dad did, though. He'd packed winter clothes for all of us. He buttoned Belle's red coat up himself." His throat rippled. "He did it so carefully, because she was still upset, telling her not to be fretful, that nothing bad would happen to his girl."

"Robert—" said Jean. Even through her anger, the naked grief on his face moved her. Whatever had happened in the estate that day, Robert had never forgiven himself for it. For a moment, the years rolled back to when they'd met again as adults, in the not-Belle world that had been left to the two of them. Then, there had been the rare glimpses of this man, the vulnerable one. It had given her hope that their marriage, driven as it was by her obsessions, would be happy. But over the years, when he continued to mask that Robert from her, from the world – from himself, even – she'd hardened to him.

"No. I need to finish this. I won't be able to face it

again." He took a deep breath, visibly settling himself. "When we reached the estate, we set off for the castle. Mum promised us something to eat in the garden. But Belle became more upset as the lough-walk went on. She asked if I could see the birds coming in over the lough and there were none.

"When we reached the estate Belle didn't want to go in. Honestly, she threw a tantrum worthy of a toddler. But Mum told her that we weren't walking all the way back to the car without a rest. Dad took her hand and half-dragged her up the driveway. I can still see her, in that stupid red coat, her heels digging in, all the way along the path. She was spooking me – us, I suppose – out by then. I'd seen her flighty. I'd never seen her scared before."

Jean could imagine the scene; the frightened Belle fighting to get free, her stressed father holding her tight. Jack had been a big man with a temper to match. Had Belle fought? Had she kicked and yelled? Or had she given in to the will of her father? Had he taken her to her death?

"What time was it by then?" asked Jean. She could imagine fingers of darkness reaching for Belle and felt sick with the depth of her imaginings.

"After lunch, for sure, because Mum gave us some hot tea and a sandwich. I ate it in about two bites, I was so hungry. When our parents' talk went back to Gran, me and Belle took ourselves off. Or, rather, mother told us to go. She told me to keep an eye on Belle." He grimaced. "I told Belle that I wanted to go along the dark walk – that's what we called the woodland part beyond the rose garden – but she said she didn't and we had a row. I told her to get lost but she stuck to me like a shadow. I put up with it, but then she started on about there being something in the woods, and got whiny. There was no sign of Finbeara. I started to think it had all been a test, nothing more, and that nothing would happen." He looked sick. "Jesus. When I look back on it.... Her whines got to me. I told her to get lost. And then I ran off, leaving her on the path."

He paused, and Jean knew he was waiting for words of comfort she didn't have. He had known Belle was scared and that Finbeara – who he had only met two days before and knew nothing about – could be waiting for her but he'd still left his little sister because she was getting on his nerves.

His hands twisted on the steering wheel, wringing it between them. "I hid and she went past me on the path. I stayed hidden – until I heard her scream."

Jean's throat closed, hotness rushing through it. A quick pain in the side of the nail, where she'd bitten it earlier, made her look down. Robert hadn't gone after his sister. He'd left her.

"And then?" she asked.

"I know what you're thinking," said Robert. He glanced at her, his face pale, part-ghoulish, part-sick. "You can think no less of me than I do myself." His words were like crystal, fragile and out of reach. "I'd never heard anything like that scream before. Nor since. Sheer terror."

"Surely you didn't ignore that?" demanded Jean. She didn't know what she'd do if he told her he had. Already anger ran through her, hot and urgent. She had to bite down to say nothing more: not until she heard what he'd done, at least.

"Of course not. I ran, following along the path she'd taken, yelling for her. I ducked under the trees, I jumped logs, I didn't slow. And then – she stopped screaming."

"Did no one else hear her?"

The investigator had never turned up any of this. It seemed only Robert had heard Belle's screams and had chosen not to tell. She could see why: last to see Belle, last to hear her and first to find her. Nausea settled, deep in her stomach. Was it possible he *had* killed his sister? That Finbeara was only a story, and it was actually Robert who had carried out the act? That he was a murderer in fact, as well as through complicity. She knew her husband to be cold; she knew he could often be cruel. But a murderer? She couldn't – quite – stretch to that.

"Not that I know of," Robert said. "Remember, this was a harsh, harsh winter. People who like that sort of weather head for the wilds. Anyone who wants to visit the garden waits for the spring when stuff actually grows. I didn't pass or hear anyone on the paths. My parents were near the formal gardens, as far as I know, and I didn't see them. I came out of the woods into the garden beside the lido. You know where I mean – the outdoor pool on the top of the boathouse?"

She did. It was a strange place, the lido, perched on a roof overlooking the lough. Even on a busy day it felt remote and secret. She'd never known if that was because she knew Belle had lost her life there, or if it was that way naturally. But she'd never liked going there, even though each year, near the start of winter, she forced herself up the small steps, head bowed, to acknowledge her friend and drop a single flower into the dark, still water.

"By then, the light had fallen. Not to full dark, but it was certainly murky. My parents weren't in sight. I learned later that they were in a blind panic, searching for us through the grounds. We must have been away for close to an hour."

Jean's breath came and went, harsh and high and dizzying. She knew how this story ended.

"Belle was standing beside the lido and as I approached I realised she wasn't alone," said Robert. "She was standing with a man, but he was misshapen. His back was bent and hunched and he had something on his head, a pointed hat, I thought at the time. His feet were odd, too, tapering to a point, like nothing I'd ever seen before. Belle hadn't noticed me and I was frightened of startling her, so close to the water, so I didn't call out."

"You never told the police this," said Jean. How could Robert have kept this hidden, despite her pleas to find out what had happened? He'd let his mother die without knowing the truth, and his father. "Or me. I've asked so many times."

He pulled over, onto the verge, and put his hazard lights on. Ahead, the road forked off into the mountains; the road they'd have to take.

"Wait. Please, Jean, hear me out." She gave a sharp nod, and he continued. "At last, Belle saw me. I expected her to run to me but she didn't. Instead, she told *me* to run. But, of course, I couldn't leave my little sister. The man held his hand out for me, and …."

"What?" asked Jean. "What happened?"

"It was the rider from Gran's garden," said Robert. "Finbeara. The Leader. Except he was different." He licked his lips. "Harder. No humour anymore. What I'd thought was a hat was a set of antlers." He swallowed. "He didn't look like a man anymore, but something that might have been one once and had been twisted and changed."

"What did he do?"

"He looked me in the eyes and his were the same. Deep. Wild. An urge built in me. I wanted to run, but not because I was scared. I wanted to hunt, to find prey and take it. My chest hurt with the wanting." He shook his head, as if trying to break the spell of forty years ago. "I forgot about Belle's scream. God help me, but I didn't care about her anymore. I reached for the leader. I wanted him to take me."

"What did he *do*?" asked Jean, her voice a whisper.

"He ordered me to bring Belle to him. He was smiling, as if it was all a game." Robert sucked in a breath. "He thanked me for bringing her like I had promised, but said I had to deliver her to him. Those were his words. *Deliver her.*"

"And?"

Robert ran his hands over his face. The hazard switch on the dashboard flashed red and then off, red and then off, showing the bleakness in his eyes.

"He touched me. His hand was cold. I couldn't pull away. I didn't want to."

"You were weak." Robert, who'd always prided himself on being strong.

He nodded, his head down. "I was. Anyone would have been. But Belle wasn't. She ran towards me, hair wild and red as her coat, but Finbeara grabbed her. His arm was so long, he surprised her. He drew her against him."

"You let the leader take her?" Jean pressed the button to lower the window. Cold air hit her face, allowing her to focus.

"No!" He grabbed Jean's hands and he was Robert, strong Robert, his hands hard-calloused from working with the horses. "I didn't mean to do anything. She grabbed for my arm and managed to twist out of Finbeara's grasp. She would have escaped, except that I threw her off me. I was in a panic, not knowing what to do. I needed her to keep going, to get down the steps and away. I couldn't go myself. I was Finbeara's, one way or another." Robert's voice dropped to a low croak. "But Belle was light and I was too rough. Her heel slipped on the ice. Her arms went out for balance, but she went down. Hard. Her head hit the edge of the pool."

"Robert....?"

He looked as sick as a person could get. He held a hand up. "Belle tumbled into the water. She sank. She didn't try to save herself."

"Didn't you *do* anything?" She could imagine Belle sinking, her red coat blossoming in the water. She thought about everything she knew about that day. None of the investigations of the tragedy had mentioned Robert being wet. "You didn't go in after her?"

"I tried to. I ran towards her, but Finbeara grabbed me and pulled me close. His breath stank. I wanted to cry at the pain as his hands dug into my arms. He drew me close, and he was nothing like the glamorous Finbeara in my gran's garden. Belle was right. He – it – was monstrous. And angry. There was no charm left, nothing but fury."

"But it didn't hurt you," said Jean. "You looked after

yourself well, it seems."

"It would have done." He was adamant, face pale. "It wanted to. But my parents appeared, running through the garden, and it dropped me. By the time they reached me, it had vanished. Before it did, I saw Finbeara clearly." His voice threatened to give. "It was another me, I realised. Another man taken by the hunt, seduced and twisted. In that moment I knew if I ever came back to their hunting ground, it would find me. So I never did. And now you know the truth. I killed Belle. I didn't mean to, but I did."

He put his hands over his face, and this time he sobbed.

A streak of light fractured the sky, mirroring Jean's broken thoughts. She had no words for her husband, nothing that would close the rift between them. She sat until Robert pulled himself together, turned on the car, and continued onto the treacherous mountain road. Amelia and Joe might already be in the estate. Now she understood the danger. It might not be a distant monster who was a danger to Amelia, but someone closer. Someone targeted by Finbeara and his troop, just as Robert had been, and who might agree another deadly trade. Someone the fae must have had at least a night to get close to, if not two, who Amelia trusted as Belle had trusted her brother. *Let Joe be stronger*, she prayed, but no one answered. Not Belle, or God, or Robert.

CHAPTER TWENTY-FIVE

The Lido (2)

JOE FOUND A battered flask, no doubt belonging to one of the gardeners, fallen at the back of under the sink. He filled it while Amelia raided her way through the remainder of the cottage's cupboards. She came up trumps with a packet of jaffa cakes that were open and a little soft but unlikely to kill anyone.

The urge to leave was strong but going unprepared could be a disaster. To get out of the mountains they needed help, which meant either finding people in the estate, or walking to the nearest village… if there was one. Without a map. In freezing temperatures. Amelia bit down a bubble of panic. Something would break their run of bad luck. It had to.

"I think that's everything," said Joe. He set his backpack down and went through it carefully. "We're good for a day at least. At least the snowmelt means we don't have to carry more water." He shrugged the backpack on. "Just don't eat the yellow stuff."

THEY LEFT THE cottage, exiting through the shattered front door. It felt like an age since Joe had broken in.

"At least it's a better day," said Joe.

Dawn had broken and a weak sun shone. The snow at the edges of the paths had begun to melt, turning crisp and thin underfoot. In the seemingly benign garden it was easy to dismiss the events of the previous night, just as Amelia always had, but this time she wouldn't. She'd had enough of lying to herself. After they got out this place, she'd tell Joe everything. Then, perhaps, she might be able to put the scared child she had once been behind her and admit that her Aunt Lucy's well-meant warnings had been garbage. Either that, or find a self-help group that she doubted existed. The thought made her smile: 'Hello, my name's Amelia, and I can see ghosts. And feel the bones of ancient bodies buried in cairns. In fact, there's no end to the weird things I've seen. Tea, anyone?"

"What's funny?" asked Joe.

"Nothing." They crunched to the bottom of the garden, the iced-over snow making her pay close attention to her steps. "Any point in trying the castle again?"

"We could have a look."

They angled towards the conservatory which stretched along the length of the castle. The main section held a formal seating area that jutted into the walled garden. Its wicker chairs looked so comfy, she almost salivated at the chance of getting in, but the door, when tried, didn't open. At the other side of the room a door that must lead into the main castle was closed. Beyond it the castle waited in darkness.

The second section of the conservatory, a long glass-lined corridor that hugged the castle's wall, contained two thin benches with young plants set along them, protected from winter frosts. Amelia pressed her nose to the cold glass, misting it with her breath. Nothing moved. No gardener came in to check the greenery. No cleaning staff, mopping and dusting.

"It's no good," said Joe. "If anyone does come in, we'll pass them on the causeway anyway."

The causeway, with the lough and its birds. They'd have to follow it again, or risk getting lost. Stalling, Amelia tried the door one last time, but it didn't give, and she had to follow Joe to the arch that led from the walled garden. She stepped through, into the turning circle for the buses.

She felt on edge immediately. Her shoulders hunched, as if she could hide. A sense of not-rightness dragged a low warning in her stomach. The trees were silent around them. No birds called, and she knew that whatever had watched yesterday still had them in its sights.

The narrow road that led to the causeway was shadowed by trees, untouched by sun and still snow-covered. No footprints broke the whiteness. Joe marched up to the castle and tried both the main door and another, set into one of the wings. Neither gave.

"It's official. We're on our own." He rejoined Amelia by the small bus shelter. She didn't know why she had stood there. It wasn't as if waiting would bring the bus. She scanned the dark trees surrounding the turning circle.

"Let's go, then," she said and trudged through the snow, towards the lough-path. Better to set off when it was light and bright, and not waste time. To their left stood a building, half-hidden in the trees, and Amelia's heart jumped in recognition.

"One second." She approached the building by taking a path shaded by close-growing bushes. The lough shone a sullen metal-dark at the bottom.

"What is it?" Joe asked. "We don't have time to traipse around."

"I know." But it was important. As she made her way down the path, her fingers tingled. Her chest tightened. The sense of Belle came to her, the Belle who had clung to her in the tree, frightened and trapped, not the older, more assured woman she had glimpsed.

"Are you okay?" Joe asked.

She was far from okay, but this – whatever *this* was – had to be faced. This was Belle's past, her story, coming at Amelia as strongly as any of her visions ever had. To run from it would be a betrayal of Belle's sacrifice in the grove.

She emerged beside what had to be the strangest building she'd seen. A folly, she supposed. It jutted into the lough, grey water lapping onto a ledge that ran the whole way around the building. It was a boathouse, she realised, but more ornate than any she'd seen, its brickwork sturdy and its green-painted windows deep set. Unhelpfully, it occurred to her that anyone could watch from its dark interior and she would never know.

Joe joined her. "What a bizarre place." He ran his hand over the rough brickwork. Darkness crept from the building, a sense of secrets. She didn't like that he was so close to the windows.

"Joe!" Her voice was too sharp, and he frowned. "Come away."

"You're the one that wanted to come down here," he

pointed out. "Look. Steps."

A set of steps ran up the outside of one of the walls and she knew where they would lead to. Even without having seen the pictures the previous night, she would have known from the sense of Belle, now all around. The news reports said her body had been found here.

"The lido," she croaked. Which ghost of the past was she seeing? One from 1945, when it had been surrounded by glamour and people, all of whom would be dead by now? Or from 1978 when a girl had fallen into the freezing water and died? "Don't go up there, Joe."

It was too late. He was already climbing. She started up behind him. The steps led to the roof of the building and, sure enough, its inset pool. No sense of its previous glamour remained. The paving around the pool was unbroken by anywhere to sit and relax. The water itself was dark and unwelcoming. The sense of something very wrong hung all around, making her head thud.

"Weird place," said Joe at her shoulder, close enough to make her jump. His sense of urgency had vanished, and she thought she knew why. There was a lethargy about this place, a separation from the real world and any of its concerns. She could have spent the day just staring at that dark water, and not cared about finding help and getting out of this estate.

"Yes. It was used by Grace Kelly, you know. She visited. And Greta Garbo. It was on one of the panels in the cottage."

She shivered. So many dead people. And not just them. All the people evicted in the famine. It had been snowing then, and bitterly cold, and they'd had to flee the mountains that encircled the lake. This estate was not a kind place. It masked itself in soft gardens and pretty buildings but here, more than anywhere, she could feel the wrongness at its core.

"Joe," she said, and her voice held an edge of warning. "We should go. No more delaying."

"You're right." He took her elbow, and his hand was too tight, making her draw in a sharp breath. His own breath was rasping. Not strong and deep as she was used to. "I don't want another night here."

Yet neither moved. The estate had lured them in yesterday: today it didn't want to let them go. Joe still stared at the water, his face half in shadow, older and leaner. His eyes scanned for something, his head cocked as if listening, and she could see the rough Joe of his youth in him. For the first time, he frightened her.

"Hey!" A voice carried in the crisp air. "Let's head to the steps and the top viewpoint."

Joe turned, the moment broken. She ducked around him, escaping his hold on her arm.

Coming up the path, towards the castle, were a group of hikers. Amelia had never been so glad to see anyone. Joe ran to the top of the steps, a wide smile on his face. She'd been stupid to feel scared of him; she'd let this place, with its secrets, infect her. She ran after him, putting the lido firmly behind her.

CHAPTER TWENTY-SIX

Re-Encounters

AMELIA WAVED AT the group of walkers, flapping her arms like an airport worker.

"Over here!" she yelled. The group stopped and responded with a wave of their own, and she hurried to the group. Joe made it down the path first, his boots' thicker tread speeding him along.

"God, it's good to see you," he said.

"Didn't expect to see anyone in here today," said one of the walkers. He was in his mid-twenties and thick-set. On his back he had a bulging backpack, as well as a set of walking sticks. He frowned at Joe, perhaps taking in the relative lack of equipment. There was nothing outdoor people liked less than people putting themselves in danger. It gave everyone a bad reputation.

"We didn't expect to end up here," said Joe. Quickly, he outlined what had happened with the car, and how they'd had to pass the night in the estate, without mentioning anything about what had happened in the gardens and woodland, which was good. Bad enough to look helpless and stupid. No need to sound like the neighbourhood kooks as well.

"You're lucky you made it to shelter," said the walker. His thick brogue marked him out as a local. He set down his backpack and pulled out two heat packs, giving a sharp snap to activate them. "Here, put those inside your coats. You look frozen."

"Thank you." Amelia took one and tucked it into her coat. The heat started to seep into her, bringing home just how cold she was. "We really need to get to a phone and arrange to the get the car pulled out."

The walker pursed his lips. "You might not be in luck with that. I think you'd need the grounds staff – there'll be no garages open today, even if they could get a recovery van through the snow. But you're welcome to call someone to come and get you, if it helps." The man fished in his pocket and pulled out a mobile in a heavy cover.

"Cheers." Joe took the phone and offered it to Amelia. "Your parents might be up for a rescue mission." A muscle ticked in his check, and neither of them mentioned that his own wouldn't. They'd stopping caring what happened to him a long time ago.

Amelia paused, thinking. Her own father would come if she called him, of course. But he'd have to travel along the atrocious roads and he wouldn't arrive much before nightfall anyway.

"Better to get some local help," she said. "The Sweeneys might know someone – that Christmas tree didn't put itself up."

"Good idea."

The reception bars were down to a single line. Amelia

walked towards the expanse of the lough. A flock of birds circled high above and she squinted to see if they were the ones from yesterday but they were too high to be sure. She shivered, despite the heat pack. She'd put money on them being the same.

The reception bars came up and, with numb fingers, she managed to get her purse out of her coat pocket. She tipped out Jean Sweeney's contact card and called the number. It answered on the second ring.

"Hi. This is Amelia King."

"Amelia! Where are you? I've been calling and calling." Mrs Sweeney's posh tones were quick, almost flustered. "You've left the cottage."

"The cottage?"

"The cottage in Donegal. Where are you?"

"How do you know?" Was this woman having her followed? Unease spiked, and Amelia wished she *had* called her dad.

"We're here. And you're not."

"You're at the cottage?" said Amelia, for Joe's benefit. "But why?"

She ignored Joe twisting a finger at his head, indicating Jean might be a bit dotty.

"We saw the forecast and were worried when you could not be reached."

More than worried, given the tightness in her voice and that made no sense. Jean must have known the weather was bad and that the reception at the cottage poor – it had said so in the welcome information – so why worry? A suspicion that had began to form when she'd first realised who Belle must be began to take a more solid shape.

"I'm surprised you came all this way," she said, finding her voice cold.

"We decided to come down and check all was well," said Jean.

They had just decided, on a whim, to travel across the country last night, when the weather had been so awful? Not just on any night, either, but Christmas.

"Tell them to come and get us," whispered Joe and Amelia nodded. Unease or not, she had no option. Jean Sweeney and her husband were better than another night in Glenveagh, facing the monsters.

"Perhaps you could help us," Amelia said. "Our car is out of action." She didn't want to tell this woman just how out of action it was, or how helpless it left her and Joe. "We need a lift."

Joe nudged her. "Or a tow. I might be able to get the car going."

He had no hope. It was a wreck. But it was Joe's pride and joy that he'd nursed through the last four MOTs and spent what little time he had away from work and the band on. She didn't have the heart to tell him to forget it and send the salvagers in instead.

"Please come," asked Amelia. "We'll be in the car park." She waited for the confirmation and then hung up, thoughts racing.

"All sorted?" asked the walker and, although he was smiling, she understood the subtext. If it wasn't, the group would have to give assistance, and that would rob them of their walking time.

"Yes." She handed the phone back to him. "Thank

you."

The walker took the phone, and the group set off, without looking back. Already, they'd be intent on their plans, not what might be happening with herself and Joe. The sun sparkled over the lough making it look benign, not cruel.

Jean Sweeney had sent Amelia here deliberately. She'd been set up. She was sure of it. They could have died last night for someone else's whim. Her temper, rarely ignited, began to rise.

CHAPTER TWENTY-SEVEN
Truths and Lies

AMELIA NO LONGER had any choice about whether to tell Joe about Belle. To not tell him, knowing they had been set up, would make her as bad as Jean Sweeney. He had been in as much danger as Amelia.

But could Amelia tell him about the other incidents, stretching back to her childhood? The thought of doing so had often wakened her at night, lying beside Joe and listening to his steady breathing, knowing that he didn't really know her and that, once he did, it might be the end of things for them. But he had seen the monsters in the garden himself and might believe her. She twisted her engagement ring. She wasn't used to it yet, how it sat on her finger, the weight of it. And she wanted to be.

Enough. Her stomach cramped, but she faced Joe at the entrance to the car park which the Sweeneys would soon drive into. She took a deep breath. She couldn't tell him about herself. She didn't have the words. But Amelia *could* tell him about what mattered.

"Joe," she said. "You know the old clippings in the

cottage?"

"Yeah."

"One of them was about a child called Belle. She fell into the pond on top of the boat house and drowned, years ago. You can look it up online, as soon as we're back."

"So? Kids die." Joe, more than anyone, knew that. Kids fell through the cracks and had accidents. Kids were neglected and died, or became drug users and died. Some made it, and some didn't. He'd been lucky; some of his friends, growing up, had not been.

"Do you remember the picture of the child in the Sweeney's house? It was the same child." He frowned, but she held up her hand, shushing his questions before they were asked. "I know it's crazy, that it sounds mad but I met her last night. Or, rather, I met her spirit." How could she make him believe? "You know last night, in the forest? Why aren't you dead from hypothermia? You slept outside, in freezing temperatures and you're fine."

"I was in a … pocket," he said.

"You weren't. You were protected by Father Daire, who was a tree spirit. I was protected by one, too, and Belle." His mouth quirked up and she knew he was going to laugh. "Please, Joe – this is important."

He sobered. "Go on."

"Joe, I see things. I always have. Things that aren't really there."

"You expect me to believe this?" He didn't sound amused anymore, but angry, as if she was taking the hand out of him.

"I hoped you might believe *me*." She touched her ring, and it felt like the only solid thing there was. "I've been like this since I was a kid, when the school took us to an old cairn and I saw the dead people."

What an understatement *that* was, to say she'd saw the dead people. They'd moved around her, in and out of vision, substantial and real and then fading, in and out, until she'd been sure she was going crazy. And all the time, her class, making noises and scaring each other and her not knowing what was real and what wasn't.

"What did you do with them?"

"I threw up," she said. Outside, on the grass, with a concerned teacher beside her. She turned away. "Look, forget it. I knew I shouldn't have told you."

Because it was crazy, and her mother was right. She should have said nothing. *That* was what she'd taken away from that day, when her mother had driven her home and her questions weren't about what Amelia had seen but who she had told, and what *they'd* said.

Joe's hand was on her shoulder. He turned her to him and she didn't fight. She looked up into his eyes, ready to see mockery, but it wasn't there.

"Is this the truth?" he asked. "Maybe you were just spooked."

"It is," she said. "I swear it, Joe." He wouldn't believe her and that would be the end of them. "Do I seem mad?"

He held up his hands, surrender-style. "Chill. No, you don't." He met her eyes. "I mean it. You're not mad. But this – this can't be true."

"I know it's hard to believe." She sat, perching at the very edge of the rock. It was freezing under her butt. "But what about last night? In the garden."

"What about it?" He sat beside her, just fitting on the

rock. His body was warm against hers, and solid.

"There were creatures there. You saw them."

"I saw something, Amelia. I don't know what it was, though."

"But you know they hunted us, right?"

"Yes... maybe." He looked frustrated. "I don't remember half of what happened." He rubbed at a mark on his wrist, and winced. "I think something bit me though."

She grabbed his wrist and brought it close to her face. The wound was long, and in two segments. Two perfect puncture marks showed within it. She rubbed her hand over it, and the skin felt cold to her touch. Her breath hitched. Another thing she didn't know, and daren't ask about, scared what it might mean. "Would you accept something weird happened?" she asked.

"Yes." He crossed his arms. "But it's a long way from that to seeing ghosts."

"I know." She fought to keep the frustration from her voice – it wouldn't help to convince him. "Look, if I'm right, Jean Sweeney knew that I might be able to see spirits." She looked down at her hands. "There was an incident, just before she contacted me. Like in Ballygally."

"A painting?" He knew about the Ballygally painting, how she hated it. He perhaps even knew that she feared it, although they'd never talked about it. Joe missed little.

She nodded. "Yes. Dark. Not nice."

"Why didn't you show me it?"

"I lost my sketchbook. I called the town hall and the police station, and it was never handed in. I had months of sketches in it." Her hands wound around each other, a pair of snakes, and she put them under her armpits to stop herself. "I wonder if someone took it and, if so, if word got back to Jean Sweeney."

"A bit of a coincidence."

"I know. Or, you know – the death was all over the papers down there." She'd looked them up online the next week, unable to stop picking the scab of what had happened. "If we were at home, I'd show you. She might have just picked the story up from them."

Except the papers had made no mention of Amelia, or even that a painter had been there. Which brought her back to Jean Sweeney targeting Amelia deliberately, having found the sketch somehow.

"Well, I had her down as kooky, so who knows? You could be right." Joe put his arm around Amelia and pulled her close and, again, she picked up a mustiness in his scent. "Look, I don't know what to say. I trust you. But what you're saying can't be real."

"Do you remember Ballygally?" she said. "You remember the state I ended up in?"

"Yes." The words between them were unspoken. It would have been impossible for him not to remember Ballygally. She'd broken down, and insisted they left before they'd even stayed the first of their three-night stay. When Joe had tried to calm her, she'd dug in even more. She could not have stayed in that hotel. Not even if someone had paid her to.

"I – something was watching me. On the beach." But that didn't come close to describing the crawling sensation, the evil, that had washed through her. "I could feel its eyes on me. Its interest in me. It brought the storm in."

"There was no one there," said Joe. "Just you and me, on the beach."

That was true. The squall had chased everyone else into their cars or over to the hotel for hot toddies.

"There *was* someone in the tower," she said. "Do you remember, I sent you up to the ghost-room to check for them?"

"It was empty, love," he said. He'd never called her that before. To use the term so casually disarmed her. Was it pity, or did he mean it? "There was no one there."

"But...." She swallowed. "In the picture, I painted her."

He frowned. "You added a figure into a picture. So what? You knew what that room was and your subconscious decided to roll with it."

She shook her head. "No, Joe. I saw the lady watching me. She reached a finger towards me and I heard her warning me to go. She called me fae-touched. She spat it at me. I knew if I were closer, she'd touch me for real." Her throat was closing. The words were hot; the memory too raw. "I thought if she did, I might die."

Joe was on his feet, wrapping her in his arms. She leaned into his chest. Telling him felt like something had left her; a hard ball of fear she hadn't realised she'd been carrying. He hugged her close and shushed her, and it wasn't until a distant swish of car-tyres made them pull apart that she realised he smelled like Joe again, with no remnant of the smell that had turned her stomach.

"All right," said Joe. "I believe you." He quirked a smile. "About some of it, anyway. Something odd *did* happen last night. I'm muzzy on what, but I'll accept that something did. And at Ballygally. I've never seen you like that before. I'm not sure what you think is what's happening, but something shook you up."

He believed her. Or, at least, he didn't disbelieve to the point of thinking she was a liar. Whether he was humouring her or not didn't matter; he hadn't rejected her. Aunt Lucy had been wrong. A lifetime of worry fell from her; she wasn't alone anymore.

Lights showed down the driveway, and a moment later a flashy Range Rover with Northern number plates pulled into the car park.

"Showtime," said Joe. "You know, if they did set you up, I will make them regret it."

His words were entirely casual but she didn't doubt him. Despite Joe's veneer of civility, once scratched he was still the child who'd learned to fight his own corner and not give a damn about others'. If you were on Joe's side, he'd protect you forever. She lifted her chin; as she'd protect him.

In tandem, they stepped to the edge of the car park. Joe took her hand and squeezed it. She'd done the right thing, telling him. With love, there had to be trust. They faced the car and she felt strong and ready.

CHAPTER TWENTY-EIGHT

Circles Within Circles

ROBERT SWEENEY'S EYES met Amelia's through the glass, unnervingly direct. Amelia thought she knew what part Jean had played in her and Joe being in the estate but Robert was an unknown quantity. Beside her husband, Jean sat in the passenger seat, face impossible to read.

"Let them come to us," murmured Joe, ever the poker player.

"Agreed," she said.

The Sweeneys got out and made their way to the front of the car, Jean slipping in the slush. Robert grabbed his wife's arm before she could fall and glared around the car park, his gaze shifting from place to place, taking in all the shadowed corners. Did that mean he knew to be wary of the estate, or was it just natural distrust? Amelia couldn't tell. She glanced at Joe and his face held the studied tolerance he used when wanting to be unreadable and remote.

"This place hasn't changed much." Robert made his

way over to Joe and Amelia. He put his hands on his hips and looked around. "So, where's this broken car of yours?"

"In a ditch," said Joe.

Amelia faced Jean. The other woman wasn't nearly as stylish as when they had last met: her clothes, whilst still clearly designer, were wrinkled and her eyes were shadowed. The Sweeneys must have driven without a stop over, and in this weather that must have been a marathon.

That decided Amelia. They had *known* something wasn't right when they had set off. *No need to allow them to be too comfortable then.*

"Who is Belle?" Amelia asked, her voice cold.

Jean's mouth opened into a small 'O' of surprise. Amelia had been right to wrong-foot her.

"Well?" Amelia demanded.

"How did you know about Belle?" asked Jean. "Did you sense her?"

Robert looked up into the trees, his action deliberate, and then back at Amelia. "And let's not bandy important names about."

He knew about the watchers. The birds and the hares and the who-knew-what-else. Not only did he know about them; he was scared. He hid it well, but it showed in the tight line of his jaw. He stared Amelia down, until she nodded: not here.

Joe stepped forwards, hands tight to his side, lightly in fists. He might not have Robert's gym-toned physique but if it came to a fight, he'd fight dirty. "Amelia asked a question. Answer her."

"Bel—" Jean bit her lip. "*She* was my best friend."

"And my sister." Robert crossed his arms, facing Joe,

two males vying for position. Honestly, they made gorillas look easy-going. "Which gives me, I believe, the biggest claim on any information about her."

How very incestuous. A missing best friend, and a husband who was her brother. Amelia tried to remember the details on the cut-out about Belle. She was sure the brother had been mentioned.

"Don't worry," said Amelia. "I didn't find out anything." Or, certainly, nothing she planned to tell these people. Her night in the forest, the magic, Belle, those were hers to know, not theirs.

A rustling came from above, followed by the sound of flapping wings. A crow took off from the trees, wheeling towards the lough.

Robert jerked his head at the car. "I suggest we go back to the cottage, where it's safe."

"Why not home?" said Joe.

"I've driven all night," said Robert. "I need a break."

"I can drive."

"You?" Robert looked Joe up and down. "You crashed your own car. I'm hardly going to let you loose with mine."

Jean grabbed his arm. "Robert. We *should* go."

He pulled his arm away. "It's fine, Jean. The cottage is safe. It still has its original doors, yes?"

"Yes. Of course."

"Then it can't be breached," said Robert. The sky had grown dark, clouds scudding over the mountains, and Amelia realised they must be into the afternoon already, what with the walk though the estate, the lido, and the long walk to the car park. "Apart from not wanting to drive, I don't think we have enough time. The hunt will be back. They will be more determined. Their time is short." He opened his car door. "And their watcher will have already told them we are here." His eyes met his wife's. "That *I* am here, Jean. They've been waiting forty years. I don't think they plan for me to leave a second time."

A shadow fell over the car park and a sharp wind sent leaves rustling across the tarmac, a rat-a-tat warning.

"He's right," said Joe. "Look at that sky. If it snows again, we'll want to be clear of the mountains. Otherwise, we risk being stranded."

"A storm will happen, if he wants it to," said Robert, with no explanation of who 'he' was. "Or a river diverted to flood the road. A rockslide, or an animal I'll swerve to avoid."

Like the hare the day before. Joe and Amelia exchanged a glance, and in Joe's eyes, she saw growing belief.

"We do not want to be stranded in these mountains tonight." Robert opened his arms, taking in the estate. "And to stay here? You do not face the hunt with nothing but guts and fire."

He knew about the hunt? Amelia hadn't expected that but to cast it out, so casually, showed that he must know they, too, knew of it. Did he know, then, that Belle had faced the hunt for years with nothing other than what he'd described?

The crow circled back towards them, its caws breaking the silence. Now was not the time, and especially not the place, to ask for more information.

"You're sure the cottage is safe?" Amelia asked.

"As sure as I can be," said Robert. "The house is bound in iron."

"What do you think?" she asked Joe. They had got into this together; they had to stay together.

"We can't stay here," he said. He was paler than earlier. Tiredness was catching up on both of them. "I don't remember a lot of last night, but I know I don't want another like it."

"Okay." Reluctantly, she got into the back of the Sweeneys' car, Joe beside her. Jean resumed her place in the passenger seat.

Robert started the car, its engine noise soft in comparison to their own car's, and they left the estate, passing through a break in the wall that surrounded it. Beyond that, the mountains enclosed them on every side. *Circles within circles*, Amelia thought, *and no way to escape beyond them*. Her skin crawled, warning her of what she already knew. They were trapped where the hunt wanted them, here in Donegal.

CHAPTER TWENTY-NINE

Trapped

THE CAR DREW up in front of the thatched cottage. Robert had driven carefully, yet quickly, but the threatened bad weather still almost beat them back to the cottage, stealing what was left of the afternoon's light, turning it to dank darkness. An outline of broken tracks led up the drive, cut by tyre wheels. She hoped Robert was right, and this place was safe. It had held firm the night she and Joe had stayed in it, anyway.

Perhaps sensing her attention, Joe looked over and gave a tired smile. On his wrist the red mark stood out. He saw where her eyes were fixed and hurriedly pulled his sleeve down to cover the mark.

"Let's get inside." Jean hurried up to the cottage, the iron key held tight in her hand. She opened the cottage's door with a twist that was almost a flourish. The hall beyond Jean sat in darkness. Amelia would have preferred to see up those stairs.

"Come on," said Joe. "Before the snow starts again."

Amelia stepped inside. The air held onto its hard

coldness after days without heat. She toggled the light switch and nothing happened; the power was still out.

"How far is it to Glenveagh?" she asked. "As the crow flies?"

"A mile maybe," said Jean. "Not much more."

Only a mile separated the cottage and the hunting ground she'd faced last night. A bird could cover a mile quickly, she bet. Especially on a stormy day with the wind to help. Amelia slammed the door so hard its thud echoed in the hallway.

"Lock it," said Robert. "Then check the windows. I'm going to use the back door and move the car around to the side and put it under the tarp. No need to announce where we are. Once we're bolted in, we should be safe."

Jean hurried up the stairs and Robert pushed past Joe, into the kitchen. He was a stocky man with the advantage of weight over the wiry Joe, who gave way without comment. A moment later, the purr of the car's engine told them he was moving it as promised.

Amelia crossed to the front window. It occurred to her that the line of fir trees that overlooked the cottage would be perfect for birds to roost in. In another half an hour, three quarters at most, the garden would be in full shadow and the house with it.

Robert returned. The sound of the kitchen door being locked, and then a bolt drawn, was sharp. When he set foot back into the living room, he looked smaller, as if Donegal had shrunk him.

"Right, let's get a fire lit." He called up the stairs: "Jean! Any candles?"

Amelia stayed by the window overlooking the front

garden, watching. Robert had said the house was safe, but she didn't feel like making any assumptions. Joe took up a similar position looking out at the back garden, standing in the lee of a small window. Amelia placed herself just inside the curtain drapes, where she could see down the driveway but would mostly hidden to anyone approaching. Her gaze tracked to the place where she'd found the prints yesterday morning, and then up to the mess outside the door. Last night, whatever had tracked the house had come closer. Regardless what Robert said about the house being safe, the garden could be breached.

Jean thumped down the stairs. "Right, all locked up." Her lips were drawn back in a smile, but it was nervous, so that too many teeth showed. Amelia couldn't decide which of the Sweeneys she disliked more. On first meeting, she'd have said Robert. He'd been so unfriendly where Jean, at least, had tried to be welcoming. Right now, he seemed the more normal.

Jean set a candle on the fireplace and a tealight holder on a side table, before perching on the end of the sofa, rabbit-tense.

"Well, then," she said. "Perhaps we should tell the guests our tale before the dark falls."

"All right." Robert lit kindling in the fireplace, making sure the wood was well lit and the fire spreading, before adding peat. He took the rocker beside the hearth. Joe leaned against the back window, close to where the curtain ended. "But, first, perhaps you could tell us what happened in the estate, Amelia? It might help with my end of the story."

"I found Belle," she said and was surprised by how

cold her voice came. "She was alone in the woods." *In a little red coat, no hat or gloves, nothing to stave off hypothermia.* "I assume she's what you hoped I'd find, Jean?"

Slowly, the other woman nodded. "Yes. I thought there might be a chance, if you *were* gifted."

Amelia's fists clenched and she wound them in the curtain to disguise her anger. "And did you know what else might be there?"

Jean shook her head. "You had the advantage of me there, I'm afraid." But her smile was still too wide, and Amelia couldn't decide if it was through nerves or evasiveness. "Although I do now, since my husband decided yesterday to share that information with me. I'm very sorry."

"So the…" Robert cleared his throat. "…the horde was there?"

"Yes." Amelia met Joe's eyes from across the room. The horde. It was a good description. "They were."

Robert rubbed his hands along the seams of his trousers. "Do they still hunt?"

"Yes." It wasn't Amelia's voice, but Joe's, croaked and low. "They do." He met Amelia's eyes, his own dark pools. "I remember that much. The horns. And the hounds."

"I thought they might," said Robert. Quickly, not wasting time, he told them about the events of his childhood and how Belle had been taken. When he finished, true darkness had fallen and the soft firelight was the only warmth.

"That's … incredible," said Joe. "And you say this – Finbeara, was it? – glamoured you. How so?"

"By the twist of an eye," said Robert. "He will find your will and take it." He stared at Joe for a long time, and it was the younger man who looked away, and Amelia felt something stab deep inside her.

"So, what happens next?" asked Jean. "How do we free Belle? That's what you need to tell us, Robert."

He shook his head. "I don't know. At the time, I could have done something. I could have offered myself in place of her. But my contract was broken the moment Belle died."

"But that's why we're here!" said Jean. "To save her."

Robert's eyes narrowed. "It's not why *I'm* here. I'm focusing on the living."

"But we must!" Jean's hands opened wide, pleading with her husband. "I've dreamt of her so often that I thought she must still be there. That she was trapped. And I was right, wasn't I?" She crossed the floor to Amelia and snatched her hands. Amelia wanted to wrench away, so cold were Jean's, but the older woman held her tightly, her nails digging into Amelia's wrist.

"That's why I brought you here. To find Belle. You're the only one that can reach her." Her eyes raked Amelia's, bright with hope. "Could you find her again? In the morning, when the hunt will be gone? Find out what I need to do to make things right for her?"

Joe stiffened at the back window, but Amelia didn't need anyone else to answer for her.

"I don't think so," she said. "Belle died last night. She gave herself to the hunt for me. I think it's over for her now, and she's at peace."

"She won't be," said Robert, his voice harsh. "It

doesn't work that way. Belle is dead, but not by the hunt's hand. She presents a game to them. No matter how many times they steal her, or how often she 'dies' again, they can't take what they want from her."

"What is it?" asked Amelia.

"Her soul. That's what they sought. The soul of a familiar, to feed on. But with Belle already dead before Finbeara took her, that soul was lost." His hands twisted again. "But she can't leave the estate, either. Not as long as my oath to Finbeara holds her there." He swallowed, and he looked terrified.

"It's not Amelia who has to go," he said. "It's me."

"But not alone," said Amelia. She couldn't leave Belle to face those monsters again. Not when Belle had rescued her. And she would not trust Robert to do the right thing when faced with Finbeara. He had been weak before; he might be again. "I'll go too. You need me to find Belle."

"Then we all go," said Joe, quickly. "I'll not let you go back there without me, Amelia."

Robert's head came up, sharply, and Amelia wondered if he'd refuse but, in the end, he shrugged. "All right."

"And me!" said Jean. "It was my idea – that we could find her."

"And you," said Robert, his voice weary. "Yes, Jean – and you."

CHAPTER THIRTY

Iron-Bound

DARKNESS FELL BUT no one left the living room to go to the bedrooms. Jean lit more candles and they, combined with the soft-red fire glow, made the room almost cosy. Outside, all was quiet. There had been no sound of the hunt, even in the distance, and nothing moved in the garden. It was easy to pretend things were normal and the knot of tension eased from Amelia's shoulders.

She moved away from the window, onto the sofa, taking the opposite end from Jean. Her eyes drooped as exhaustion threatened to pull her under. At the other end of the room, Joe still stood guard over his small window, an occasional cigarette glowing in the darkness. No one had objected; going outside was not in the picture.

A knocking sound came from outside the front window, jarring Amelia awake. "What was that?"

Robert was on his feet straight away, his hand up in a shushing gesture. "Quiet. They may try to flush us out."

"Nothing out here," said Joe. Jean had grabbed the end

of the sofa, her knuckles white.

No need to ask what *they* were. Amelia strained to hear anything more, but things had gone quiet. The clock ticked on and on, a heartbeat to the cottage.

"Might just be something in the wind," said Robert, but Amelia couldn't sit, blind and passive, waiting for something to happen.

Quietly, she moved back to the front window, shifting the curtain so that she could see out. She pushed her face into the gap between the curtain and window. The brickwork smelt musty and old and the curtains as if they'd been hung before they were fully dry, giving a sour, dense smell. Nothing moved in the garden. It *had* been a false alarm. Amelia let the curtain fall back into place.

The window behind Joe crashed inwards.

"Jesus!" He jumped away from the shower of glass. Cold air invaded the room, a shriek of wind accompanying it. A wizened hand crawled around the sill, more claw than human, seeking purchase. It grabbed Joe's coat-tail, and he tried to wrench the hand off, but it only tightened further.

Robert launched himself at the arm. With a snarl, the monster pulled itself onto the sill, black leather-skinned, as big as a man. Amelia cast around, searching for anything that could be used as a weapon. Suddenly, she remembered the window beside her and jumped away, barely in time: a bang shook the window frame; claws scraped along the glass. The hand drew back and crashed against the glass, creating a crazy-paving cracked pattern.

Amelia darted into the centre of the room. Robert had hold of the creature gripping Joe and was wrestling with it, his arms stretched out to keep its fangs, hissing and biting, from his face. Blood seeped down his wrist, onto his hand, following taut lines of sinew. Joe tried to break free, but couldn't dislodge the creature.

"Here!" For all her hand-twisting earlier, Jean seemed commendably composed. She grabbed the fire poker and tossed it to Amelia, before picking up the shovel and hefting it. With a yell, she ran at the creature attacking her husband and brought the shovel down, hard. It threw its head back and squealed. A stench, perhaps old leather, perhaps bone, filled the room.

Joe staggered away from the window. The creature had backed into the corner, eyeing Jean warily. Robert joined her, one hand covering the long gash on his arm.

A crash behind Amelia told her the second window had been breached. "Upstairs!" she yelled. She held the poker in front of her. Jean joined her, hands tight on the shovel. Joe snatched up a second poker for the fireplace. It briefly crossed Amelia's mind to wonder who needed more than one poker. Robert took an iron spike from its place adorning the wall. It was at least eight inches in length, sharpened to a fine point, and made a decent weapon.

They backed to the hall, first Amelia and Jean, then Robert, with Joe bringing up the rear in a low crouch. More creatures entered the room through the open windows. Joe feinted at them with the poker and the creatures cringed back, hissing. Up close, they were horrifying, wizened, their stench a putrid smell of decay that Amelia half recognised, although she didn't know from where. One snatched at Joe, stunningly quick and bold. It dug its claws into his arms, but he ducked back before it could get a grip and, with a yell, broke free. Blood pooled where the claws had been. He, too, ran for the hall.

Jean stopped onto the third step, poker in hand. Amelia took the step below. Robert joined her, panting heavily, one hand holding the spike, the other curled around his bicep. Blood seeped from his wound.

Joe hefted the poker. "Come on, then, big boys," he said. He didn't seem to have noticed his own wound. In fact, he seemed to be enjoying himself. "Let's see what you're made of."

Two of the creatures advanced, growling. They dwarfed Joe and their reach was longer, but they stayed back, eyes on the poker.

"Don't like this, eh?" taunted Joe, feinting with it.

More of the creatures came into the hall. There was something human in the twist of their mouths when threatened by the poker, in their watchful eyes. Amelia took a step down, dull with fear, and joined Joe. A quick thud of feet behind her made Amelia glance back to see that Jean had fled. Amelia couldn't decide whether to feel sorry for her fear, or hate her cowardice.

The creatures advanced, swerving to avoid the darts of Joe's poker. Their mouths were curled back in low snarls. One snatched upwards and Joe feinted, but barely avoided a counterattack. Joe jabbed again. The creature's eyes followed the poker's movements.

Cat-swift, it grabbed it and howled. The smell was sickening, but the creature held on, trying to wrench the poker from Joe's grasp. It pulled him to the edge of the step with a sharp jerk that nearly had him off his feet.

"Get off!" Amelia brought her poker down, hard, on the creature's forearm. If Joe was pulled into that swell of monsters, he would be lost, as he had been the previous night.

The creature yelled and loosened its grip but more were behind it, flooding into the hall, and Amelia and Joe were forced up a step, and then another, pushing Robert back, too.

"What now?" muttered Joe. "Any ideas?"

Nothing, except staying out of reach and that wouldn't work for much longer: they were running out of stairs.

"Just one." The voice came from above, imperious and rich, much more like the Jean Sweeney that Amelia had first met. She came down the stairs, pushing past Robert, joining Amelia and Joe on the step below. In her hands she held two horseshoes that must once have belonged to a cart horse, they were so big.

"They forget how long this house has been here, and how close it is to their hunting ground. I bought it off a couple who had lived here for years and they told me –" She held the horseshoes out "– to always keep iron in the house. And this is worked iron, forged to tame an animal. The strongest there is." She lunged forward, wielding the shoes. "Begone! This house is bound in iron. It's in the doors. It *was* in the window frames before I replaced them. More fool me, thinking I knew better." She thrust again.

A creature hissed up at her, snarling, eyes intent, but it made no further move towards them.

"Be careful," said Joe.

Jean laughed. "They'll not tackle these. The people I bought this house from knew what they were doing."

She lunged forwards and the fae fell back, their faces twisted.

"Gran's house was iron-clad, too," said Robert. He raised his spike and it, too, had a sense of age that the pokers did not. "We claim this house. Leave."

Snarling, the fairies retreated. They avoided the door, studded with iron bolts and the heavy iron lock, and backed into the living room, herded by Jean and Robert, Amelia and Joe using their own weapons to stop any breaking from the pack. The creatures climbed out through the front window, dropping down to the garden to fade into the night. Jean set one horseshoe on the windowsill, and the second on the back sill, where the window had been breached.

"What now?" Amelia asked. It felt wrong to let the creatures go but there had been no way to defeat them all. Not with so many. She still held the poker in her hands; now, she realised the tip was loose. She could have been let down by it the night before. Carefully, she unscrewed the end and put it in her pocket, not entirely sure why, just that it felt safer to have it on her.

Robert looked weary. "They're waiting for us to come out."

"But they can't take us in the day?" she asked.

"No." His eyes didn't leave the window. Joe, his poker held high, watched at the other. "But they are not without influence, especially during their High Moon. They will not be helpless, even in the light." His face was grim and Amelia's nerves jangled. She wanted to be far away from the Sweeneys, not brought into whatever their game was but things – whatever they were – had gone too far for that.

CHAPTER THIRTY-ONE
The Return

AS THE NIGHT drew on, Amelia would not have believed it was possible to exist on so little sleep, and it had made her faintly nauseous. She crossed her arms over her chest, trying to ease the chill that invaded her.

"Amelia." Joe's voice, soft as it was, made her jump. "Why don't you get some rest?"

"I can't," she said.

"You could try." He took her by the shoulders, rubbing the top of her arms and bringing some warmth. "Come on, I will too. The creatures won't come back, this close to daybreak. Plus, Robert will keep watch."

"I will," said Robert. "I took an hour's kip earlier."

He had, too, snoring on the sofa. Amelia had envied him the ability to do so. Jean had dozed, too, taking the chair by the fireplace.

"Sit down," said Joe, and Amelia sank onto the sofa. He was right. She – *they* – couldn't go on without rest.

"You, too," she said.

Jean took up position at the back window, Robert at

the front. Amelia watched for a while, but both Sweeneys remained alert, and her eyes began to droop. Joe curled up in the armchair, his coat wrapped around him, and closed his eyes.

Somehow, Amelia slept until Joe woke her with a gentle shake. Her mouth was dry and her mind slow, too deep in sleep to come quickly alert. Her dreams had been vivid: of being chased, of monsters in the house, and the garden under bright moonlight. She stretched and her joints clicked, but she made herself get up and go to the back window. The rush of freezing air brought her round. The horseshoe was still on the windowsill. It seemed a flimsy protection but it had worked.

Gradually, the sky lightened. A streak of pink on the horizon warned her that the weather would be inclement, not kind, and that made her shiver. Jean drew the curtains at the other side of the room, juddering them along the rail, and perched on the windowsill. Her clothes were still immaculate, her designer jeans hugging legs tucked into boots that must have cost hundreds of pounds, but her makeup had smudged. Her hairstyle, too, was less than polished.

"All right," said Robert. "Planning time, everyone."

A sharp spasm in her side made Amelia wince, but it was nothing other than muscles held too tight. She was going to do it. Go back to the estate and try to reclaim Belle from the hunt.

"Sun's almost up," Robert said. "We need to get some food into us and then hit the road. It'll be a long day, and we need to keep our strength up."

"I'm on it," said Jean. "We keep some stocks for

welcome packs in the housekeeping cupboard."

"Joe, you get the car ready." Robert had assumed command without it having been discussed. Was that because Belle was his sister or that he seemed most sure of himself?

"Right you are," said Joe. He stepped towards the front door, stopping first to watch out the window. "You're sure all is quiet out there?"

"There's been nothing around the cottage for the last hour or so," said Robert. "They'll be returning to their lairs."

"I'll come with you." Amelia picked up the poker, comforted by its weight and the cold, dead feel of it in her hand. "I can do the battering."

"Excellent," said Joe. "I always like a woman who can batter."

"I need you to check the wheels and have a look in the engine," said Robert. "See if anything has been tampered with. Turn the engine over and run her for some time."

"You think they'd know what to do with the car?" asked Amelia. How could the creatures be so smart? In the forest, yes, where they dwelt and hunted, but with city things? Surely paranoia was creeping in.

"I think they'd do anything to take us down. If they thought they could get to us more easily here, they might do." Robert tipped his head to the sky, as if something might appear. "They're cleverer than you know."

"But we can hold them off," said Amelia, hefting the poker. Not that she wanted another night like this one.

Robert pointed at the ceiling. "We can hold them off from inside the house. But what about a bird overhead, dropping a burning ember into the thatch? What if the wind was just so, and caught it? The house would go up. And when we have no house? And they come in greater numbers?"

"Would they be so clever?" asked Amelia.

"Yes. We must be prepared. And that includes choosing our hunting ground, our own plan, and our agenda."

"We hear you." Joe opened the door, letting a further flood of cold air in. "You keep guard, Amelia. Yell if anything moves."

They exited. The light was just enough to see by but Amelia had to strain to make any detail out. She took up position at the corner of the house, where she had a view over the garden and the approach up the driveway.

Joe made his way to the car. She heard his steps as he walked around it, followed by the dull thump of the bonnet being lifted. Next, the muffled sound of the engine and the heavy smell of petrol reached her. She realised she'd been holding her breath, sure something would have happened the moment he started the car. It rumbled on and on and nothing exploded.

The engine stopped. Joe crunched back to her.

"Is it my imagination or is it getting foggy?" he asked. "I can barely see the end of the drive."

He was right. It had come down gradually as she'd been waiting, a silent blanket that now surrounded them.

"I don't like it," said Joe. "Snow to trap us, then clear skies while they hunted. Why this?"

"I don't know." To keep them at the cottage, perhaps? Or to turn them around in the mountains so they would be unsheltered as night fell?

She led the way back to the house, but paused in the doorway. The fog weaved around her, fingers of white reaching for her that hadn't been there even moments ago. She pulled back, as if it could actually grab her, and slammed the door.

"Right," said Robert. He stood in front of the dead fireplace. Silently, Jean handed around brioche rolls, the long-date type that smelled almost artificially sweet, and black coffee. "I believe if I give myself to Finbeara, that may be the end of things. My pact with them will be fulfilled: one of us to hunt, me or Belle." He swallowed, his throat rippling. "That's the easiest way to solve this and your roles are to witness the oath so that it's binding, and to bring Belle to that binding. Then, Finbeara can free her."

"Except you don't know it will work," said Jean. She did not, Amelia noticed, protest at her husband's proposed sacrifice, only at the practicalities. She was a cold woman, in her perfect clothes, masked from Amelia's understanding. Amelia wished the Sweeneys had never turned up; that her and Joe had been left to get rescued by the walkers and dumped in Letterkenny to make their own way home.

"We can't allow that," said Joe. "We go in together, and we come out together."

"It doesn't stop the hunt, anyway," said Amelia. She willed Jean to say something, to behave normally and try to find a way to keep her husband safe, but the other woman just stared out of the window with an impossible to read expression. "Is there another way? One that could finish the hunt forever?"

"There is something else we could try," said Robert. He drew something from his back pocket, which unfolded into a map of the estate. "Listen up. This is how."

CHAPTER THIRTY-TWO

Cast and Agreed

JOE DROVE, WITHOUT any discussion. Each person had fallen into their role easily, and without argument. Jean had the most recent knowledge of the area and, therefore, took the passenger seat, the better to navigate through the mist. Robert sat in the back, overseeing all.

And Amelia? She, too, sat in the back seat, nerves jangling, every vein in her body pumping with the knowledge that things were not right, that going back to the estate was, without doubt, a trap. The closing in of the mist convinced her of that. If the others had their areas of specialism, perhaps her intuition, driven by what she could not see but only sense, was hers. In which case, her instinct wasn't helpful; telling everyone not to go into the estate, to keep driving and not look back, wouldn't help Belle.

Robert stretched up and curled his fingers around the roof's hand-hold, muscles bunched and ready. If it was possible, he looked even more tense than Amelia felt, as if he would jump out of the car at any moment. He, too, knew the hunt and what they were capable of. It was possible, given his family's ability, that he could also sense what couldn't be seen.

As they drove, the mist eddied and swirled. The sign for the estate's turn off appeared through a thin patch of mist; the trees on either side of its driveway were shrouded sentinels. Anything could be within.

Carefully, hunched forwards, Joe turned the car onto the driveway. Briefly, the gash left from last night's attack became visible when his sleeve stretched and lifted up. It felt like they were being carried into another world. Amelia found her breath half-held.

"There's no back way to the castle?" asked Joe. "Might be worth trying? Because we're sitting ducks on that causeway."

"None that offer any more cover, that I know of," said Robert. "Jean?"

She shook her head.

"We can't risk getting lost," said Robert. "Even if we could see enough to go off road, the hunt could still pick us up. They don't watch entrances and exits. They watch from the sky and the forest."

And by feel. Amelia was sure that just as she could sense them, the hunt would feel the car entering the estate and track them by that knowledge and not by sight. She pressed her forehead against the window. Something moved in the whiteness, a grey shifting shape that she could not make out the detail of. It seemed to keep pace with the car. Silently, Amelia pointed at it, and Robert nodded.

Joe drew to a halt at the estate entrance's expansive car

park. The road ahead led to a barrier, Amelia knew.

"Any ideas?" asked Joe. "There must be a way onto the causeway with a car – there's a bus stop at the castle."

"They're parked beyond the barrier, I expect," said Robert.

Once again, they were where the hunt wanted them to be. In the estate and exposed. In a moment, they'd have to make it along the causeway. The walk would take an hour, at least, and all the time they'd be tracked. Before they even reached the castle and its maze-like grounds, any watchers would know exactly where they were.

"Joe's right." Jean's eyes were sharp. She might act the posh poseur to perfection, but Amelia felt sure that a truer self lay hidden under the designer clothes and perfect hair. She wished the other woman was not there, that she'd stayed back at the cottage; her presence jangled Amelia's nerves.

"In what way?" asked Robert. "Do you know another way in?"

"No. But we don't need to take the car." Jean tapped Joe's shoulder. "I assume you might know how to hot-wire a vehicle? You seem the type."

Joe stiffened, the old defences about his background showing. If asked, he'd express no shame about his years on an estate, running wild prior to being fostered. But the family who'd brought him up through his teens had taken the edge off his roughness and provided enough nurturing for him to grow distant from his childhood. Amelia could see him struggling with the question, but he managed to get past his annoyance, and nodded, a single wary nod. "If I have to."

"Yes, you seemed very good with cars," said Jean, and it was hard to tell if that was what she had meant all along, or if it had been a jibe at some rough edges she had sensed in Joe. "I thought we could take one of the estate buses. The ones that take the tourists down to the castle. They must be kept where there is access to the causeway."

"You want me to steal a bus?" asked Joe. "Who's paying for this after? I mean, they've already got me for breaking and entering."

Amelia almost smiled at Joe's optimistic assumption of there being an 'after'. Someone had to believe.

"Don't worry about that," said Robert, evidently more pragmatic about their chances. "We can sort that out. Can you do it?"

"Probably," said Joe. "But do we all want to?"

"I'm in," Amelia said. They couldn't afford to worry about small things like criminal damage. The hunt wouldn't, after all. "It's a great idea, Jean."

Jean flushed at the compliment.

JOE PARKED IN the shadow of the trees at the far end of the car park, away from the couple of vehicles already parked up, presumably belonging to more hardy walkers. He left the car well under a canopy of thick, overhanging branches.

They got out. Amelia closed the door behind her, its metal smooth under her hand. It clunked shut: even with the care she'd taken, the noise was loud in the otherwise silent car park. Incongruously, Joe locked the car before handing Robert the keys. They shook loose some twigs to land on the bonnet, making it hard to tell that the car had only just arrived.

"All ready?" asked Robert. At murmurs of agreement, he squared his shoulders. "Good. Let's go. Stay together: me and Jean; Amelia and Joe. Don't let the person in front of you go out of sight; if the fog gets thicker again, we could lose each other easily. Remember, stay in our teams all the way."

The short trek across the car park felt hideously exposed. Unsurprisingly, the mist lifted. The snow, too, had begun to melt, but around the edges the tarmac remained white and shrouded. They crept around the side of the Visitor's Centre to where a dark, narrow, iced-over footpath stretched towards the lough. It led through bunched evergreens, with no breaks between them. The sense of being herded was again unmistakable and Amelia bunched closer to Joe, seeking the security of numbers.

At the bottom of the path, a turning circle matched the one at the castle. In it, three buses were parked up. The group were forced into single file at the end of the path, so that they emerged one by one: Robert at the front, then Jean and Amelia, with Joe bringing up the rear.

"Which one?" asked Amelia, to Joe.

"Whichever's easiest," he said. "Or, even better…." He pointed to a small van had been parked behind the buses. Less obtrusive than the buses, it looked like something maintenance might use even on a day the estate was closed. "Are you all prepared to slum it and pile in the back?"

Joe didn't wait for an answer, but made his way over and tried the driver's door. He gave a short laugh when it opened. "Guess it's not crime central around here." He got in, and felt behind the sun visor, but his hand came away empty. "That was too much to ask. Damn Terminator. Everyone knows not to leave keys there anymore."

Amelia climbed into the back of the van, clambering over a set of shears, left open so that they yawned at her. The van held a whiff of manure, making her nose wrinkle, with the sweeter smell of grass below it.

Robert crouched beside her. "Try not to attract any attention. Keep your thoughts off the hunt, if you can. That used to be Belle's downfall: she couldn't keep her mind quiet. No wonder they found her."

His words had an edge that she didn't like. A dismissiveness about his sister, and herself; a sense that this might be all their fault.

"Got it!" said Joe. The van started up. "Let's get this baby on the road."

Amelia's mouth went dry. A part of her had hoped that this wouldn't work, that the van would not start and they would decide to call off going further into the estate, back to the hunting grounds.

The van moved off sharply, nearly sending her tumbling. She steadied herself and tried to distract her mind, but she was tense, half-expecting to hear the thud of something landing on the roof or the squawk of a watcher. Through the back windows the lough glinted as they joined the causeway. The watchers would not miss the van. Surely, they'd see past the ruse. They drove on for long minutes, following the causeway. Dread filled Amelia. She wanted to turn back. She should turn back. And yet she would not.

At last, they stopped. Joe looked into the back and found Amelia, his eyes to her eyes. "We stick together. This place feels different." He screwed his face into a grimace. "If I'm feeling jumpy, it'll be off the radar for you."

She clambered into the front seat, leaving the Sweeneys to sort themselves out in the back.

Joe had parked in front of the castle. There was a dankness in the air, a sense of hunching darkness. She pulled the door handle and got out. Fear hit her, so hard that she doubled over with a low groan. Sweat broke between her shoulder blades, finding it difficult to breathe.

She forced herself to straighten. If something had focused so hard on her, they must see her as a threat. She managed a breath, counting in and slowly letting it out. She focused on the chill of the air, not its weight around her, and the sound of the wind in the trees. At last, she gathered herself enough to be able to take in their surroundings.

The snow had melted in patches, giving a dappled look to the place, but a mist made the tree branches appear to be reaching for her. Goosepimples puckered the skin along her arms.

"Remember, we stick together," said Joe. "Right?"

She nodded. Robert joined them. A slight twitch in his cheek above his tight jaw the only thing to tell her that he, too, had picked up the atmosphere. He was limping slightly, she noticed, presumably a remnant from the night before. Shadows appeared to form around him, as if he was another focus and pivot. His sister had been a sensitive. Was he, too? His supercilious comment from earlier, warning her not to attract attention was ironic, given it was he that drew the shadows. Jean emerged from the van, brushing down her trousers, and she paused in the circle, looking all around her.

With a squawking and rattle of wings, birds rose from the forest, long beaked and sharp eyed. They swooped and screamed, pinpointing the van's position.

"Go!" Robert said. A bird dived for him, and he ducked away. He grabbed Jean's hand. "You know what to do, Amelia. Get going!"

They'd gone over their planned actions that morning. They were cast-hard and agree, but she hadn't expected this headlong run. Already, the day felt like it was unravelling.

Amelia and Joe took off, sprinting towards the walled garden and the woodland path that led to Mother Beith's grove.

Amelia took one look back as she ducked through the gate. Robert and Jean had stayed behind, ready to face whatever approached from the lough, just as planned. She hadn't expected them to look so small under the canopy of trees, the watching water behind them.

Small, and helpless.

CHAPTER THIRTY-THREE

What's Love Got to Do with Anything?

"WHY DID YOU tell them to run?" asked Jean. "There's nothing here."

Nothing except a flock of birds circling. No fairies or monsters. Nothing like what Robert had described. Her dreams had been so vivid, these gardens so full of promise, she felt betrayed.

"The birds," snapped Robert.

"But they're nothing but crows," she said.

"They're fae," said Robert. "The horde come in from the west, often in disguise." He stared upwards, grim-faced. "Or they could just be their watchers. Or nothing. That's the worst of all this. Things could be something or nothing. It's how Finbeara lures people in. By seeming like nothing dangerous." He squinted. "Do they really look like crows to you?"

She stared at the circling birds, cawing to each other. "Of course."

"Not to me," he said. "I can see what they really are

and they're nothing like crows, no matter what they're projecting."

Jealously stabbed Jean. If Robert was telling the truth, he could see the world that she could not. The same world Amelia and Belle could see. Even Joe had seen something the previous night. She felt like a child again, frumpy and useless against the ethereal Belle who took everyone's attention.

The birds circled overhead and there *was* something in the way they flew that made her uneasy. The too-perfect circle never moved away from herself and Robert, but kept them within.

"What do they want?" she asked, but she already knew the answer.

"Me." Robert's voice carried no inflection. He appeared accepting of his fate. "I had a pact with the fae and I broke it. They will want redress."

"But you brought Belle to them," she said. This was what she could not understand. Finbeara had caused Belle's death, just as much as Robert had. He'd frightened her – and how she must have been frightened – into bolting. That Robert had been the one to push her, and the one to betray her made him a murderer, but Finbeara's hands were not clean either. "You fulfilled your pact."

"But then she died." His voice was matter of fact. He'd betrayed his sister, and she had died. Ancient history, not a raw wound that ate at him as it did Jean. His eyes were hard as he watched the birds, not paying any attention to Jean, his posture tight-wound. "That wasn't what I promised. A dead soul. But it's what I delivered." His lips thinned. "Although the outcome was the same. She was dead whatever happened that day."

For the first time, it occurred to Jean how alone they were. If she yelled, there would be no one close enough to hear. By now, Amelia and Joe would be deep into the forest and well beyond earshot.

"What *did* you promise?" she asked. This story from him differed from what he'd told her in the car.

"I promised them prey, so that I could join the hunt." His posture remained tense, his shoulders back, his stare fixed. "The hunt do not allow their prey to live." He met her eyes. "Ever. Once Belle was dead someone else had to become their prey or her spirit would be trapped forever. That would have been me, but for my parents. Today –"

"I know," she said. "Today you'll let them take you and free Belle." Her hand lay at her throat. It rippled under her skin. She struggled to breathe.

"They will not take me," he said. He looked up at the birds, still circling. "Not when there is better prey to be had."

Jean took a step back. If she ran, would she escape? But she knew the answer. Robert was fit. He'd taken part in an Iron Man for charity a few months ago; he rode every day. She did Pilates once a week. He'd take her in just a few steps.

"What do you mean?" she asked, voice staccato with fear. "What better prey?"

He must have noticed her moving away, because he laughed. "Not you, Jean. You can't even see the watchers. What fun would you be to the horde when they hunt? Besides, they can take someone like you anytime they like. No, they bargained for someone fae-touched. It makes for better sport. If I give them that, my bargain still stands."

Fae-touched. As Belle had been. As Amelia was.

"You can't," she said. She needed to get away, to warn them. "Amelia didn't even know why she was here!"

"Well, if you will play with fire.... You should never have brought her here. I told you to leave this place alone, and you wouldn't listen. I tried to forget about the pact, and the hunt. God knows, I've tried to stay away. But – knowing you had placed *her* here? Another fae-touched? Knowing I'd get to join the hunt after all, not be taken by them. I'm only human, you know." He spread his arms out and tilted his face skyward. "Hey there! Tell your master to come to me. Tell Finbeara I can give him what he wants." His smile widened. "Tell him he can feast tonight."

Jean ran. Dashing to the side, out of reach. Towards the arch into the walled garden. One step, two steps, then five. She was going to make it –

His hand grabbed her arm, tightening like a vice.

"I can't allow you to leave, I'm afraid," said Robert. He turned her around, and started to march her in the opposite direction.

"You're a bastard," she said.

"I am, at that." Robert forced her down a shaded path to their right. Its narrowness gave no room for her to twist free. The lough glittered dully at the bottom, where the path opened out. Beside the water stood the stone boathouse, its brickwork jutting into the lough. "Like you always knew."

Jean struggled to free herself. He'd killed Belle close to here, at the lido on the boathouse roof; what was to stop him repeating the act?

The lough lapped at the front and sides of the building, partially covering the concrete walkway that ran around it. Its water hit with a dull warning, and the first line of escape was closed to her. If she fell in, she'd be lost in moments. The water was too cold to survive.

"Get back!" said Robert. "Away from the edge."

He yanked her backwards, and she lost her footing. As she slipped, his hold loosened, and she was able to twist free. She dashed around him and back up the path, but he was too close behind her and she'd never make it. Her hood was pulled back and she added a burst of speed to break free. She dashed to her left, up the steps. If the gate at the top was open, she might be able to close him out.

She reached the top. A stiff wind blew off the lough, bitterly cold. It tugged at the buttons of her coat, as if seeking to expose her. The dark pool of the lido – where, summer after summer she'd pilgrimaged to remember Belle – mocked her in its dark stillness.

"For God's sake, Jean," said Robert. He was out of breath, she noted with pleasure. "You can't be up here."

He snagged her wrist and pulled her to him. For years, she'd imagined her friend dying at the pool, her red coat dragging her into the darkness. How scared she must have been. Now, she knew the same fear.

"Robert," she said. "Don't do this." She knew her pleas wouldn't stop him. If forty years away hadn't broken the spell Finbeara had cast, her words could not. "If you ever loved me, don't do this."

"Of course I loved you."

Something rushed through her, a relief that she hadn't been a fool, that there had been something between them.

It mattered more than she'd thought it would. Even here, betrayed, it still mattered, and she hated that it did.

"I still do."

He shoved her, to the edge of the platform opposite the lough, just above a lawn. The edge of the walkway went from under her. Jean grabbed empty air, hands flailing. Her mouth opened, but the scream did not come. She hit the ground, hard, and everything went black.

CHAPTER THIRTY-FOUR

The Shape of the Trap

AMELIA GRABBED JOE'S hand. The birds overhead were watchers; she could feel their attention on her. Even without the agreed-upon action, she would have fled: she could not stay a sitting-duck, waiting for Finbeara – if the Hunt-leader she had viewed last night was indeed him – to return.

She tracked along the back of the conservatory, aiming for the rose garden with its bare branches. Circles within circles, walls holding walls. She tried to see the pattern and work out how she could utilise it, but could not.

The gate that led into the dark forest path was closed again. Amelia put her hand on the heavy lock, and the terror of last night flashed back to her. Would she face the same horror tonight? If so, would they – Finbeara's daytime watchers in the woods – trap her and Joe somehow, holding them until nightfall? It was, she was sure, what the hare had tried to do yesterday. Force them off the road, to where they would have been easy to overcome. And the trap wouldn't be hard to set in the wilderness. Creeping vines could capture either her or Joe, or trip them up so that they broke an ankle. The mist could thicken once more, turning them around in the woods until night fell.

"What's wrong?" asked Joe. "Let's go through."

"Just… thoughts," she said. Damn her too-vivid imagination. "Let's go."

She twisted the handle and pushed the gate open to show the dark woodland path waiting beyond. Joe passed through, and she closed the gate behind them. It gave a dull thud, like clods on a coffin.

"Where to now?" asked Joe. "This is your show." He gave a quick grin. "I spent my night under a tree, remember?"

She did. She also remembered the blood around Finbeara's mouth. Her eyes strayed to Joe's wrist, but he had his coat's cuff unfolded so that the mark was hidden.

She'd been sure, in the cottage when they had planned this, she would be able to find her way back to the grove where she'd last seen Belle. But now, faced with the tangled woodland, it wasn't so straightforward. To find the grove, she had to find the ward Belle had used. To find the ward, she had to take the right path. If she could not, they were beaten before they began. She stopped at the first fork in the path, unsure what to do.

"Amelia," said Joe, softly. "We aren't going to find what we need standing here."

"I know. This way." She led the way to the set of steps Belle had taken her up. *All right, then. One step at a time.* She began to climb. The steps went on and on, an endless twisting to the next flight, and then the next.

"You do know where you're going?" asked Joe, breathing heavily. "First thing I'm doing when we get back is getting off the smokes." He smiled up at her. "If you're going to turn into some sort of crazy-lady, taking me in and out of magical forests, I need to get fit."

It felt like there were more steps than the previous night, but she couldn't be sure. Then, she'd had the adrenalin of the chase running through her. She could have been climbing for hours and never known it. Perhaps she should sniff the air or something and see if that helped. Robert had promised to draw the hunt away long enough for her to find the grove and Belle, and here she was, lost and useless.

At last, she reached a break in the steps, and she really didn't know where to go next. A faint breeze lifted Amelia's fringe. It carried a warm smell that gave a sense of safety and retreat. She arched her back, easing its complaints from the climb. Two paths led off, one carrying her further up, the other branching to the right, along an earth-ridge. The breeze strengthened, and she turned with purpose to the ridge. "This way."

The ridge quickly became overgrown. This wasn't a true path, laid out for the visitors who came to the garden, but wilder and secret. A branch lay across the trail, just the right size to beat the brambles back with. She picked it up with a quick murmur of thanks, embarrassed at her superstition. But if the forest spirits *were* helping, it would do no harm to show gratitude. She beat back the brambles that encroached, making sure not to touch the trees above.

Grey stone shone from below, barely visible. Excitement leaped in her, but she tried to stay calm. This estate was years old, it would have more than one fallen wall in its grounds. She used the stick to beat her way to the stone and saw it *was* a low wall that formed one side of a ruined building. She had come at it from a different angle, but she felt sure it was the building where Belle had placed the ward. It looked right but, more importantly, it *felt* right.

"This is it." She held her hand out to Joe as they navigated the steep slope down to the clearing. The scree was loose underfoot and it would take little to overbalance and tumble down.

"Stay with me when we go into the ruins," Amelia said. She didn't know what would happen when she stepped over the wall. She hoped it would lead to the grove, but it was just as likely they'd just step into a ruined building and that would be that. Or, that she'd carry them somewhere entirely unexpected. Or, even, that she'd vanish and leave Joe behind. Both her and Belle had the magic – or whatever it was – needed to cross the wards. He may not.

"Oh I will." Joe breathed the words, and she glanced sharply at him. He took her hand, his own warm and dry, and tightened his fingers around hers. His breath was still tight from the climb. It had been that, and nothing more.

She stopped in front of the wall, and brought to mind the grove and Mother Beith. She closed her eyes and, with her free hand, traced the shape of the tree, detailing where the face had been and where the slender limbs had shown. A peace grew in her, oddly combined with the excitement of what she might be able to do. She tightened her hold on Joe and, together, they stepped over the wall into the ruins.

Something lurched, deep in her stomach. She staggered forwards, pulling Joe with her. The air felt lighter. A sweet-smelling breeze surrounded her. Gingerly, barely daring to hope, she opened her eyes and found herself in the same ruined building, holding Joe's hand, in the same forest.

"Damn it." They needed her to be able to work the wards, to do what the others could not. "Sorry, Joe. It's not work—"

Her words fell away. There, in the middle of the surrounding walls, the grove of birch trees appeared, shimmered, and then disappeared. She took a step forwards, breath held, and focused on where the grove had been. The image returned. This time it grew stronger and steadied. In its centre stood Mother Beith, her trunk writhing and changing: a body this moment, the hint of a face the next.

Amelia ran to the tree-spirit, taking care not to tread on any roots. It felt like coming home, to know the tree had survived the battle in the grove, that she was untouched by the evil. Amelia put her arms around the trunk, feeling the slashed lines under her hand, cheek on gnarled bark.

"Mother Beith," she said, barely moving her lips. "I came back. I brought Belle's brother with me. He's at the castle. He thinks there might be a way to free her."

Free her – free her, the tree seemed to breathe. Its branches swished viciously, making the sound of an engine.

"Do you know where she is?" Amelia asked. "Can you show me?" She strove to stay calm and not let her sense of urgency escape into the air around her. If they were to get to Belle before nightfall and the return of the hunt, she must be quick. Already, the afternoon must be stretching and she remembered how quickly darkness had fallen the day before. “Belle’s friend came, too. Jean. And Joe. Father Daire helped him, like you said he might.”

Joe stepped forwards. “Hi.”

The bark grew cold against her cheek. Amelia drew back.

“Mother Beith?” Amelia let go of the trunk. She remembered how the tree had fought the fairies, impaling them on its sharp branches. It had been a ferocious fight. The grove no longer felt like a place of safety.

“What’s wrong?” asked Joe.

“Stay back,” she said. Even Belle had treated the tree with respect. “I don’t know what’s the matter.” But something was. The air fizzed with anger.

A branch whipped through the air. Joe yelled and jumped to the side, but the sharp end caught him, trailing along his cheek, snagging him deeply enough to draw blood. Another came at him and he barely avoided what would have been a heavy blow to the head.

“Stop!” yelled Amelia. “He’s with me!”

The trees crowded around them, blocking the way out. Another branch lunged and Joe jumped to the side but Mother Beith moved quicker. The tree captured Joe. He yelled as a branch wound into his hair and pulled him against the trunk.

“What’s happening?” Joe’s head was wrenched to the side. His cheek pressed flat against the wood, so that his face scrunched up. Another branch whipped around his throat. He tried to bring a hand up to pull it away, but his limbs were held and it was useless.

Amelia darted forwards, reaching for the whipped branch. She wriggled her fingers around it and pulled, but it didn't move. Joe's face had darkened to a deep red; when he heaved a breath in, it was rasped and forced.

"Stop!" said Amelia. "Mother Beith. You must stop."

"She will not," said a new voice. "She can taste the monsters' taint on him. He cannot be allowed to stay in the forest."

A woman stepped into the glade, gracefully slipping between two of the trees. She wore a long red dress, against which a fall of dark hair hung to her waist. She stopped in front of Mother Beith. "Well done." She traced her fingers along the slashed marks in the wood. "This promises safety." She put her hands on her hip, coquettish and oddly familiar. "And allowing the fae's followers into the forest isn't safe."

"He's not the fae's!" shouted Amelia. "He's Joe. Just Joe."

Just Joe, who had faced the forest with her. Whose eyes were half-closed, his hands dragging on the branch that choked him, exposing the mark on his wrist.

"He's one of them," said the dark-haired woman. "They've taken his blood." She reached for Amelia's wrist, and turned it up, so that a mark from the brambles the previous night was visible. "Just as I took yours. Just a nip. That's all it needs."

"Belle?" Amelia asked. The woman had the same colouring. The dress matched the child's red coat.

"Of course." The woman dipped her head in

acknowledgement. She wasn't just older. Her face was thinner and longer, but also more composed. Her now-tidy hair no longer wild and tangled as it had been. If there had been a study in how to look regal, this would be it. Amelia found her hands dropping to her side, as if seeking a skirt so she could curtsey.

"Please," Amelia said, her voice choked. "Let Joe go. He's done nothing wrong."

"That's what he'd have you believe." Belle's face hardened, but she snapped her fingers. "Very well. You can have it from his own mouth."

The branches holding Joe drew back. He collapsed to the ground on all fours, shoulders heaving. Belle walked around him, so that she stood behind him, and she stared down, eyes like stone.

"Well, man. Can you hear me?"

Joe lifted his head. Slowly, he nodded.

"And do you know me?"

He shook his head.

"Liar." She pursed her lips. "Tell me, then. Did you meet a man in the forest? A man you liked, who promised you much?"

"I can't remember," said Joe. He looked at Amelia, and then away, but she'd seen all she had needed to. He *had* met Finbeara, just as Robert had. The betrayal went to the core of her. "I dreamed of him, I think."

Even when Robert had told his story, about the fae-king and how he made him feel, about how he'd been enchanted but had hidden it from Belle, she hadn't doubted Joe. Even knowing that Finbeara had feasted on something in the forest, and seeing the bite on Joe, she had believed. He was Joe, strong in himself, not weak and easily swayed. And yet it seemed he had been.

"Why?" she asked. "Why not tell me?"

But she knew the answer. He had not forgotten his night in the forest. He had not forgotten Finbeara and whatever the fairy-king had asked of Joe. He just hadn't been able to tell her.

Her blood ran cold as she saw the shape of the trap that had been set for her.

CHAPTER THIRTY-FIVE

Tumbling Down

JEAN WOKE TO a thudding in her head. The hard ground had robbed the last of her warmth. She shifted, trying to get up, but yelped at a sharp pain in her shoulder. Carefully, not quite sure what had happened, she opened her eyes, and found herself lying under some deep foliage. Above her, a fir tree stretched up the sky.

She closed her eyes and ordered herself to think. With a sense of quiet horror, she began to remember. Robert had shoved her off the edge of the boathouse. He'd told her he loved her, and then he'd pushed her. None of it made any sense – there had been no foliage where she had fallen. And she and Robert had hated each other with more passion than they'd ever loved.

She forced herself to sit up, ignoring various jolts of pain, but was none the wiser about her surroundings. Somewhere in the estate, presumably. Helpless, wherever Robert had put her.

She turned, carefully, and pushed up onto her knees. A wave of dizziness hit and she had to wait, head down, until it passed. When she lifted her head again, she couldn't see Robert anywhere in sight. Nor the boathouse or lough.

She managed to get to her feet and rest in a low crouch. The ground swam beneath her, at once solid and then uncertain. Slowly, still low to the ground, she made her way through the undergrowth, emerging a few feet away from a turret which stood alone in a garden to the side of the castle. Much plainer than the castle, without any of the artistry of the boathouse, the turret was nevertheless solidly built and sturdy.

She limped to it and ducked inside the brick-lined entranceway, hitting her shoulder off the wall. The interior of the turret was shadowed, untouched by the sunlight, and its brickwork cold when she touched it. Some crisp leaves had gathered against one wall, where the wind must have pushed them and held them firm. A metal staircase twisted up the inside. She could see through the rungs and was sure – or as sure as she could be in the gloom – that no one waited in the darkness above her.

From the top, she'd have a view across the estate, able to see anything that moved. More importantly, she'd be able to see Robert. She couldn't believe that he'd drawn her into believing him. She'd been convinced for years that he'd killed Belle and all it had taken was him to open up and tell believable lies for her to be sucked in. She deserved to be in this position. She deserved to be dead, for being so stupid. Next time, she'd be ready for him. She had to be, for Amelia and Belle; she shuddered when she remembered his words about what kind of prey the hunt might seek.

Jean put her foot on the first step. Clumsily, her head woolly, she climbed. The steps clanged and she worried someone would hear her, but when she emerged at the top, all around remained quiet and still.

She leant against the wall. Her hand brushed stone, grainy and sharp, and she took comfort in how real it felt. She stood like that as the afternoon sun began to fall in a winter-quick tumble towards dusk. Still no one moved below: not Amelia and Joe from the deeper wood, as planned; not Robert, seeking her; not the supposed-fae. Just Jean. Alone, cold, and scared, standing in plain view of the lough and its watchers.

CHAPTER THIRTY-SIX

The Lost Child

BELLE LOOMED OVER Joe, barely recognisable as the lost child who'd embraced Amelia the previous night, with her dimpled face and warm manner. This woman was both beautiful and cold in equal measure, and there was nothing ethereal about her. She looked as solid as Joe, who glared back at her, uncowed.

"You think I don't know when a man has been touched by Finbeara?" Belle gestured around her. "I'm trapped here because a man was turned by the King."

Joe tried to move away, but Belle lashed out with her foot, her kick whippet-quick. It impacted with a sharp, dull thud. Joe crumpled, clutching his thigh, but he didn't make a sound.

"You are dirt to me," said Belle. "And you will not take Amelia for Finbeara, either."

"Stop!" Amelia said. "We don't know what happened. Let Joe speak." At least let him have a chance to explain himself. Robert, when telling his story last night, had told a very different one from that of Belle. He'd tried to save her, not kill her, in the end.

Amelia stepped forward, ready to confront Belle but a branch wove around her wrist. She tried to shake it off, but it tightened on her until she grimaced.

"Stay there, filth," Belle said, touching Joe with her foot again. "Your woman might not know what you are, but I do. Unclean. Touched. The magic here is older than me. It knows the danger.

"When this grove was planted, Mother Beith was a sapling. Now she's gnarled and twisted and fears the wind might snap her branches. Father Daire doesn't roam further than the third ward any longer. He has no greenwood. He could not have protected you last night. But the hunt?" She looked at Amelia, almost pityingly. "They are hungrier than ever. The old ways are lost. They grow stronger, unbound by iron and unchallenged by those who would contain them."

Joe got onto his hands and knees. "The fae have nothing to do with me." He raised his head, meeting Amelia's eyes through hair that had matted to his forehead. "If it wasn't a dream – and I think it was – I *did* meet the man Belle's talking about. I met him after the hunt passed and you were gone. He promised me anything I dreamt of, as she says. He asked to meet him tonight, again, this time with you. I said no." He scuttled to the side when Belle gave a hissed warning and raised her foot. "I told him I wanted nothing."

Then why hadn't Joe told Amelia about this encounter? Why hide it, when she'd told him everything?

"And yet you were so coy," said Belle. She flashed a smile at Amelia as if reassuring her that what she did not feel able to ask, Belle would. That she was strong enough to. "Why was that, fae-man?"

"Because *nothing* happened. It was in the middle of the night, I was scared and sore, and I was sure it was a dream. He offered. I declined. I didn't make any deal."

"And when Robert told us what happened to him, didn't you guess it might be real?" asked Amelia. She wanted to believe Joe, but it was too convenient.

"I thought it might be." He lifted his chin. "But it doesn't matter. I refused. He left, and your Father Daire sheltered me. I curled up at its foot, expecting not to open my eyes again. And when I woke this morning, the memory was hazy. It still is."

"You lie," Belle said. Amelia shivered as familiar fingers darted up and down her spine in warning, joining her building headache. The same fingers that alerted her to danger no others could see. What had she unleashed in coming here? What was Belle, really, and what did she intend?

The trees had crowded the grove. A branch reached for Joe, who drew away.

"I've done nothing!" he said. "Amelia. You know me better than this. You know I wouldn't side with anyone who wanted to harm you."

Amelia looked between Belle and Joe. She didn't believe Joe would knowingly endanger her, but Robert had talked about how the fairies had glamoured him. How would she know if Joe had been affected too? He could be protesting his innocence and as much under their spell as Robert had been when he tried to hand Belle to them. The grove waited in silence, and she knew it waited for her.

"I believe him," she said, at last. She faced Belle. "I do. I ask you to free him."

"Then you are a fool. He carries Finbeara's marks. He is of the king."

"But it is my choice," said Amelia. "Just as you had to decide whether to trust your brother."

Belle's face hardened. "I never trusted Robert. And nor should you trust this man." The branch unwound from Amelia's arm. "Take your filth, if you must."

What sort of fool had Amelia been, thinking Belle was different to every other creature that dwelt in this forest? That she was innocent, or unknowing just because she was a child? Belle had spent 40 years in the forest.

"He is your creature," said Belle, her eyes hard. "I have no claim on him."

Joe got to his feet, shaking off the remaining bindings. He glared at Belle, his eyes flashing. "I'm no one's creature."

"So feral," she laughed. "You will be a great addition to the hunt when they claim you." She glanced at Amelia. "And you will be the price he pays to join it." She placed a hand on Amelia's arm, her touch cold and hard like marble. "The hunt is not kind to the men it claims. Finbeara will take him and use him, and hurt him until he is wizened and lost as the other hunters are. My way would be quicker, if you allowed me to have him."

She was talking about killing Joe. He stared across at Amelia. *Believe me*, his eyes pleaded. *I did not do it.* But Belle's words circled, and Robert's of that morning, and the moment held for too long, and she did not know which of them to trust.

CHAPTER THIRTY-SEVEN
A Displacement of Blackness

JEAN TENSED AS a howl carried from the direction of the terraced garden, followed by drumming hooves. She strained her eyes but could pick out nothing in the gloom. The tower that had presented safety in daylight would be no use in the dark and she'd delayed long enough.

She put her hand on the railing, preparing to descend, but shuffling in the darkness below her made her stop. It *could* be the leaves in the entranceway, but the sound had a furtive quality that set her on edge. She imagined she could hear breaths, too, as if someone was inhaling with their mouth open to make the noise quieter.

"Who's there?" she asked. "Robert, is that you?"

There was no other way down. Too late, she realised that if anything had found its way into the turret, she was trapped.

A movement beyond the stairs took her attention; a shadow in the garden, little more than a displacement of blackness which could be something or nothing. It stalked towards the tower. She spun and behind her, coming from the direction of the castle, there were more movements.

Rustling came from below, again. She shrank back against the cold, old brickwork as the sound of steps on metal matched the dull thuds of her fear.

CHAPTER THIRTY-EIGHT

Forty Years

ROBERT STARED PAST the lido's dark water. The place hadn't changed in forty years. Sure, there were nice bus circles and signage, and the visitor's centre was new, but that was just window dressing on the true heart of Glenveagh. Beneath it, the estate remained the same. It still sent fingers of dread through him, tightening his chest and shoulders, making him bite back a groan.

He leaned on the parapet, making sure he could be seen easily from the lough. Every part of his body ached. The memory of the Iron Man contest, not two months ago, felt unreal. He could not imagine being that man again, able to run, to cycle, to be so alive. The estate had stripped any vitality he had, preparing him for Finbeara. But he'd had forty more years of a good life that he should not have had. Forty years had to be enough, surely. At least, too, he'd moved Jean – the fall had been mere feet, not enough to endanger her life – to somewhere she would not be found. She would never forgive him but, by removing her from sight, he might have saved her life.

Finbeara's pack would have broken her in moments, an entree to the prey they really savoured.

He'd told Amelia, that morning, that he could break his pact with Finbeara. Forty years had given him the strength, he'd said, and she had believed him. Hell, he'd almost believe himself even though, unlike a woman, he knew Finbeara's touch, and what he could do. A hundred years would not have placated the king or made him inclined to forgive.

But coming back to the estate, feeling its hard-edged air, had eroded his resolve, reminding him of his younger self. Back then, he'd wanted the glamour of being a hunter. He'd wanted to live forever, to not know the weight of older bones pulling him to his death.

But there was no escape. He didn't care about escape anymore, only that he wouldn't be given to Finbeara's hounds, his body pushed to exhaustion before the hunt fell on him. He'd be ripped apart, teeth rending and tearing, dragged over the ground to Finbeara who would steal his heart and leave Robert's cold body lying for the carrion beasts to pick over.

To escape, Robert would have to gift Finbeara Amelia King, in place of Belle. Another fae-touched. Even if she was not connected to Robert – the King liked prey who were linked to his hunters, it made them richer – he didn't believe Finbeara could refuse. So much talent: she would last a long time for the hunt and, unlike Belle, she would be alive, her body pliable and able to be broken. When Finbeara ate her heart, he'd take all her talent into himself and further increase his own power.

If he squinted, Robert could reimagine Belle's red coat billowing up to the top of the water before her weight pulled it down. The coat turned from red, to brown, to nothing, and Robert had stood, frozen, knowing what must happen. The King did not want a corpse; he'd wanted Belle's vitality, her spirit. Her connection to Robert, his hunter, that made the kill the more satisfying. But most of all, he'd wanted her gift. Robert, with one clumsy movement, had stolen that from the Fae-king just as surely as he'd stolen Belle's life when he'd tried to save her at the end, when the enormity of what Finbeara asked became real.

His breath quickened. He relived that day, looking for the cracks in time when he could have changed what happened. How he'd turned to the king, his arms spread and pleading, even as his sister's body had been taken by the water. Should he have dived in, instead? Or called for his parents? Would any of that have changed things?

"I didn't mean it," he'd said. His voice had broken, and he'd hated how that showed his fear to the king, who wanted brave warriors not weaklings. "It shouldn't have happened."

He'd repeated that refrain to himself for forty years: it shouldn't have happened; it was an accident; Belle should not have died.

The fairy-king had grabbed him. Bony hands; long fingers. He'd been pulled against Finbeara in a grotesque embrace. Even now, so many years on, the smell of his breath was vivid, the carrion stink of old blood and death.

The glamour had been ripped from Robert then, and he'd seen what really lay ahead if he became a hunter. Not the excitement he'd dreamed of, but instead the slow death of what he was. Robert would be lost to the hunger that came.

His chest heaved, as if he was still that child. Sweat lay in the hollow of his throat, pooled and cold. He should have died that day. He would have if his father had not rescued him, sending Finbeara deep into the estate, never to be spoken of again. That had been the day he'd learned his father was fae-touched. Today, he had only himself, and his gifts ran shallow, not deep as Belle's had been. He could not save himself without a sacrifice to satisfy his debt.

But, perhaps, saving himself was not worth that price. Perhaps he was not worth *any* price. Fear eating at him, Robert made himself stand still. He spread his arms wide and heaved a breath so that he would not disgrace himself with a timid, terrified, whisper. He'd done that once before; he would not again.

"Finbeara!" he called, and he was proud of himself because it was strong and soared over the grounds. "I'm here!"

On his own. No Jean, who Finbeara might take to use as leverage. No Amelia to tempt Robert; she was lost in the gardens, most likely unable to find her way through the wards. It was a hard skill to master.

Now, here, it was just himself, Finbeara and the hunt. Perhaps the end would not be so bad. Perhaps there would be some cold glory in knowing he'd robbed the king, even as he was ripped apart.

He shivered with the cold knowledge that he was lying to himself. He was terrified, nothing more, nothing less. But still he stood, waiting for the king to come out of the forest.

He waited until he heard the scream that broke his hope.

CHAPTER THIRTY-NINE

Carnal Knowledge

A LOW, FEARFUL moan escaped Jean's lips. Something *was* climbing the stairs, its steps a rat-tat threat. She ran her hand along the wall, seeking anything that could be used as a weapon: a loose stone, or a chunk of concrete, but she found nothing.

She kept her eyes on where the staircase emerged. Perhaps she could get past, and down the tower. She sidled around the top of the platform, being sure to stay away from the staircase, and took up guard behind the steps. The one advantage she had was that the hunter would not know her position on the platform.

A figure appeared at the top of the stairs. Tall, and broad, its head hunched forwards. Too tall for a woman. Not the right stature for either Joe or Robert. It must surely be one of the creatures Robert had described.

Jean slipped her hand into her jacket pocket, readying herself.

That small movement was enough to give her away. The creature snarled and lunged for her. She screamed and darted backwards. It was so fast. She ripped her hand from her pocket. In it, she clasped the mace spray Robert had once bought her. At the time, she'd thought he was being ironic – who would want to attack frumpy little Jean, after all – but she was glad of the gift now. She brought it up in a wide spray, catching the creature full on the face. It staggered back, hands clawing.

She ran for the steps and sprinted down first one, then, two, and then down and down. She could see the bottom. Twice her feet slipped on the metal. She didn't look behind, but down, always down. And then she was at the bottom, the ground solid under her feet. She ducked out of the tower and into the garden's wide darkness.

A long, low horn call greeted her, from not far away, and she stumbled, unsure where to go. There could be anything in the shadows that surrounded her.

Behind her came a low laugh. Around her, shapes formed out of the darkness, low to the ground. Something snarled in the darkness. A cold finger touched the back of her neck, lifting her hair like a lover. The mace spray dropped from her hand and she spun, knowing what – who – must be there.

The fae-king was taller than she'd imagined, and more monstrous than even her dreams had shown her. She had to crane her head back to take in Finbeara's face, wizened and cracked by age. His smell hit her, the stench of the once-human body decomposing into itself.

"Well, now," it said, voice rasping through her bones. "I think the boy-man hoped we would not find you…"

It grabbed and twisted her, so that a clear, sharp line of

pain rushed through her, chest to stomach, down her arms, into her fingers, through her legs to her toes.

This time, Jean didn't scream. This time, she shrieked.

CHAPTER FORTY

Wards Into Wards

AMELIA STEPPED INTO the centre of the grove, her decision made. Belle's eyes were intent on her. The scratch on Amelia's wrist burned, reminding her of what Belle had said; that she'd marked Amelia just as Finbeara had Joe. Did this mean Amelia was joined to Belle, as Robert had been Finbeara's? She knew nothing about who Belle really was, how she had survived here, or what she wanted. She didn't even know if Belle was a girl, or the woman she'd fleetingly seen, who'd then been hidden again. Had she decided to trust Belle because she was a child, without asking herself questions about who she really was?

All the more reason to get away, *right now*. Amelia focused on the sense of the garden they'd been hunted in last night. Joe's hand rested lightly against hers, neither making claim nor plea. The trees surrounded them in a tight ring; the air had become too close, almost dense. More circles within circles, enclosures set within enclosures, entrapping her. This was Mother's Beith's ward, its magic stronger than any. She had no idea how to be free.

And yet, the hunt had broken into it last night, whilst her own ward had held them at bay.

"Belle," Amelia said. Surer of herself, she met the child's eyes and, this time, she could see the woman within, her dark eyes filled with cold knowingness. "I'm leaving."

She grabbed Joe's hand and imagined the fireplace in the Gardener's Cottage, focusing on the dark smell that had come from it and the rustling sound of wind through papers. That was her ward, Belle had said. Surely, she should be able to find it.

"No!" yelled Belle. She lunged forwards, hands reaching like claws. With a sickening swirl, the grove vanished and Amelia slammed back into the cottage. She lay, stunned, in front of the fireplace, Joe's hand caught tight within hers.

"What the—?" said Joe.

"I did it," Amelia whispered. She had worked magic, and it had done what she demanded; taken her from the grove to here, where she was safe.

Joe blinked and took in where he was.

"Thank you," he croaked. "You believed in me."

So many hadn't, throughout his life. Written off by his school, by his neglectful parents, by so many, Joe rarely expected people to see the best in him. Only his foster parents had, for too short a time, too late.

"I'm sorry," he said. "I should have told you about the dream." A frown crossed his face. He took his hand away from hers and got to his feet, his movements urgent. "I don't know what sort of stunt this magical king can pull. Given what your friend Belle just managed, we can't take the chance." He planted his feet. "I'm staying here until you get out of the estate. I'll follow you in the morning, when it's safe."

He didn't say the words, but she knew what he was thinking: if he saw the morning. If this place was even safe.

She, too, got to her feet. She was shaky as hell, depleted by the magic but it didn't matter. She had done it. Not as she had this morning, when she'd used Belle's already opened ward, but by claiming her own and forcing her will to it.

"Joe," she said. "I'm not going anywhere without you. I *know* you. You will not hurt me." She reached for his hand, and took it again. "Now, let's go and find Jean and Robert and get out of here."

"What about Belle?"

She shook her head. "We can't do anything about Belle. This estate holds her, as much as Finbeara."

But not here, in this cottage that Amelia had claimed for herself. And not the grove, where Belle had to ask permission for each action within it. Where, then, was Belle's ward, where she was safe? And Finbeara's?

"How so?"

"She took me to that grove last night, just as he found you. She took me there, and she filled me with so much rubbish, about her wards and her magic." Still, he was frowning, still he didn't understand. "That grove belongs to Mother Beith. Belle showed me nothing of her own ward. She showed me nothing that was real, and hers. I don't know why, but last night was a sham. A game of her making. And I'm not playing any game I don't know the rules of. Especially not here. We get Jean and Robert, and we get out. Together."

Joe held her gaze for long moments, and she thought she might have to stand her ground. But in here, in her own place, she was confident she could. At last, he nodded.

"All right," he said. "But if our friend Finbeara shows himself, you leave me. Agreed?"

"Agreed," she lied. Joe seemed so calm about everything. He hadn't even known there was a fae-world until yesterday, and today he was taking it all in his stride. She wished she could be so calm. Instead, she felt like she'd throw up at any moment.

"Let's go and find the Sweeneys, then," he said. "Before it gets any later."

"If they're still here," said Amelia. "They might have left."

A scream cut through the air, high-pitched and fearful.

"Oh, hell," said Joe. "They're here, all right. That was Jean."

"It came from the estate," said Amelia, taking off at a run, Joe beside her. She raced down the garden, not caring what watched, reaching the archway, coming out into the empty turning circle. Amelia knew where this night was going to end; where it had to end. "The lido."

A horn blared, close by. Thundering hooves made the ground shake. The full moon appeared from behind a cloud, already working its night's charm. Amelia put her head down and ran like she never had before, thankful for the rapidness of the melting snow that allowed her feet to be more sure, onto the path leading to the boathouse.

"Jesus. It's all kicking off," panted Joe. "All for one, and all that there....?"

"Has to be." They climbed the stairs. At the top, Robert waited on one side of the lido, caught between two creatures. Jean was at the far end of the pool, held tight against a dark, tall, monster.

"That's him," said Joe. "Finbeara." Awe tinged his voice, a timbre Amelia didn't recognise as his. "The king."

So he did know him. It hadn't been a dream. Fear licked at the edges of Amelia's resolve, but she dampened it down. Fear was what Finbeara wanted; what he fed off.

"Bring her to me," said the king.

"Leave me," said Joe. His voice cracked. Amelia backed away.

Something stopped her escape, something dark and unyielding. Amelia turned to leave, but a second monster had blocked the steps.

"I said. *Bring her to me.*" The king's voice was iron-hard. Amelia couldn't imagine anyone having the strength to refuse him.

Joe reached for Amelia. Blood ran from the cut on his wrist to his hand, tracking his sinews and tendons as if the blood itself was alive. He grabbed her arm and led her forwards.

She tried to shake free. "Joe! Let me go."

But he didn't. He couldn't. She turned her face from the king's stench. Jean's eyes searched hers, desperate and pained. The claws holding her loosened and the creature let her go. She fell to the ground, bonelessly.

"We will hunt well tonight. And then we will feast." Finbeara smiled, a wide slash of horror. "Once we have dispatched our traitor. We can feed him to the hounds."

"I will not fight you," said Robert, his words through gritted teeth. "But let those who are not part of this go."

"You think I wanted you? Is that why you stayed away?" The king shook its head, pitying. "You failed once. You are sullied. You are not worthy of the hunt. Besides, I have another." The fairy-king beckoned to Joe. "Your life for another's, we agreed. I claim my prize. The fae-touched are the finest to hunt."

Amelia waited for Joe to refuse, to deny the king, but it did not come. Belle had been right. There had been a meeting and an agreement. Amelia had been a fool not to listen: Belle had survived the hunt for 40 years. She knew more about this place and its rules than Amelia ever would.

"Joe," she said, and her voice caught. She would not beg.

He ignored her and stepped forwards to the creature. He bowed his head: Joe, who bowed to no one.

Robert struggled to free himself. "Take me, damn you. I'm fae-touched. I give myself."

"Silence!" The king twisted its hands in the air. With a single hard wrench, Robert fell to the ground, his body twisted. "You are nothing."

Joe, head bowed, stood before the king. His hands were clawed into fists. Sweat beaded his temples but still he stood. Finbeara, a smile of triumph on his face, waited. He was enjoying the moment, the bastard. Amelia could not move away; the creature behind gave her no chance to do so.

Finbeara reached for her. Joe did not stop him. Amelia could not stop him. The Sweeneys lay on the ground and she thought they might be dead. The king's finger touched her neck and Amelia fought not to flinch. The tip was cold, and sharp. It would cut her skin like butter. She lifted her chin. Met Joe's eyes.

"I trust you."

The finger tracked along her cheek. Robert came to, blinking blearily, but the fight had been knocked out of him. Amelia bit her lip, determined not to make a sound. No begging, no pleading.

Joe raised his head. His dark eyes held Amelia's gaze. His neck was corded in tight tendons.

"No," he told the king. "I will not agree. You cannot take her."

Finbeara's lips drew back, showing a line of sharpened teeth. "You deny *me*?" His free hand shot forward, reaching for Joe.

A ripping noise sounded from behind Amelia. It felt like her fillings could shatter, as if her bones could break. She turned. A single ripple which broke the surface of the lido and spread before it settled. In the middle of the pond, the older Belle stood, impossibly tall. Water ran off her but when it hit the pool, the surface did not ripple further.

"You may not have her," she said. She gave a smile, and it made Amelia want to turn away, so cruel was it. "I have marked her already."

The sound of slapping water came from the lough. The wind rose around Amelia, carrying the heavy smell of water and the sweetness of the mountains that ringed the estate and held it close.

Finbeara's face curled, as if in pain. He put his hands to his head and squeezed. "We must have our prey. We hunger."

"It is not permitted."

The wind grew, becoming a roaring. From the trees, a black crowd took flight birds flapping and crowing to one another.

"You have no claim. You cannot take mine." Belle pointed at Robert. "Take that and leave. He will have to suffice for you."

Amelia was sure the king would refuse, that he would overcome Belle but, with a tearing cry, he turned away. The wind howled around him, picking at his garments. He staggered back. He looked smaller, more wizened. Two of his monsters pulled Robert to his feet, who didn't fight but stayed between them.

"Belle," Robert said. "For what it's worth, I'm sorry."

And then he was gone, taken down the steps to where the hunt waited, his footsteps fading into the night. A moment later, the horns went up.

Joe ran to the edge of the platform. "He'll die! We can't let them take him."

Belle raised her arms. Droplets fell from her elbows, into the water which stayed still, like a dark heart that couldn't be touched.

"I can't help him," she said and her eyes took in Amelia's. "Whilst I'm held, I cannot stop the hunt."

Walls within walls. A pool, surrounded by stone paving, surrounded by a stone parapet. A ward of water and stone, that smelt of the underworld, of broken carrion flesh.

"You can't leave," said Amelia.

Joe joined her at the edge of the pool. He looked down its length; the water's still surface. Jean tottered unsteadily over, her face shocked and Amelia couldn't tell how much of the evening she understood. Did she realise that, even now, her husband would be fleeing for his life as the hounds pursued him? No doubt Finbeara's pack would stretch the hunt out and make a game of it whilst Robert, terrified, exhausted, would be forced to run and run.

"What can we do?" Jean asked. "I brought her here to help you. That's what you told me, in the dreams."

Belle looked at Amelia and no one else. "I wanted you to free me." She slapped the water and the surface didn't ripple but sat, rock-steady. "I hoped you would open another ward and take me through it," she said. "But you took it for yourself, and here I still am."

In Finbeara's ward. Trapped, to be hunted by him and played with, only to be returned here each night to begin the hunt again. His toy. Robert's misery would end tonight. But Belle's?

The child-woman stood, encased in the water, surrounded by stone.

Amelia felt in her right pocket, her fingers closing around the hard tip of the poker. Slowly, she removed it from her pocket.

Belle's eyes widened as Amelia lifted her hand. "You make deals," she said. "I would make one with you tonight." A hound howled in the distance. "Stop the hunt. You know the forest and estate. You could save him."

"Why would I? He killed me."

It was Jean who stepped forwards, the wife who'd never seemed to love her husband, the cold woman Amelia had never understood.

"He's not a good man," she said. "God knows, I know that. But he doesn't deserve this, Belle. Not when it was Finbeara who turned him." Another howl went up, and she winced. "Please, Belle. I did everything you asked of me. I brought what you needed, did what you haunted me to. Now I ask this of you. Don't let another of your family die because of what happened the night you… died." She had choked on her words. She looked so thin, standing at the edge of the pool, her hair bedraggled, her makeup smeared, clothes torn and ruined. "Let you have peace, and him. And us; let us know that we didn't do what *he* wants and deal out more death. Let us not feed Finbeara's evil."

A slow smile spread over Belle's lips and it was the smile of the child she had been the night before.

"I suppose I could lead the hunt a merry dance. You could take my brother as I lead them from him."

"Your promise," said Amelia.

Belle raised her chin. "I promise to be hunted once more, to give you the chance to take my brother. I can promise no more; the hunt is Finbeara's to command, not mine." The smile danced. "But he will not catch me, and you will have time. The Hunt will go to sleep hungry."

It had to be enough. Amelia threw the spike. It hit the water with a crash, and the water splintered. Amelia covered her ears and fell to her knees as a squealing noise came from the pool.

Belle's face contorted. A scream trailed from her lips,

long and high and awful. The surrounds of the pond cracked. Water flowed around Amelia's ankles, over the edge of the boathouse and down, into the garden.

Belle strode to the edge of the boathouse and stared down into the garden. Her eyes swept over it, taking in the hunt. At last she nodded, satisfied, and turned back.

She was a child again. Long hair, red coat; the same child who had been lost in the forest.

"Thank you," she said to Amelia, to Joe, to Jean. And then she jumped, into the gardens, and was gone.

Below them, in the garden, from where Belle had melted, someone appeared, walking towards the lido with a limp.

"Robert!" Jean dashed for the steps and down, racing over the grass to her husband.

Joe looked over at Amelia. "I say we get out of here."

The hunter's horn sounded in the distance. Hooves drummed. The hunt hunted.

Amelia put her hand in Joe's. Her ring pressed hard against her finger.

"All of us," she said. "Together."

EPILOGUE

"GO ON THEN. Show me." Joe sprawled on the bed, kicking his boots off into a practised double flip.

"Watch." Amelia took sand from a bowl on the sideboard and spread it in a circle around her. She imagined the noise of the gulls, the swell of the water, the briny edge to the air. It was difficult, to make the scene vividly enough, but with practice, the knack was coming a little easier. "Ta-da."

The room shimmered. The floor turned to sand, the wall to water. Gulls circled overhead.

"Can you see it?" she asked.

Joe sat up. His eyes circled around. "Jesus. That's amazing."

"I'm not very good yet," she said. Sweat broke on her brow. With her toe, she rubbed the circle, breaking it. The illusion fell away. "But I'm getting better."

"And Robert taught you this?"

"No. His grandmother." She lifted the battered book from the sideboard beside the bowl of dust. "She wrote down how her spells worked. For Belle. Robert gave them to me. He's been very patient with me."

"But what use is it?" asked Joe. "I mean, it's very nice, a trip to the seaside. But we can't eat it."

"I thought," she said, and felt the redness rising to her cheek. Would Joe understand how important this was to her? "I thought I could learn to use it to help people."

"How?"

"By finding out what people need to know. Like I did for Jean, when I found Belle. I thought, when I get more control, I might see hidden things more clearly. In fact…." She handed him the business card she'd made up. "What do you think?"

"Amelia King, psychic artist," he read. He gave a low laugh. "Well, it's different."

"Do you think it's daft?" Because she wanted to do it. She'd wanted to ever since she'd returned to Glenveagh. The lido had been repaired and it felt lighter, peaceful. Returned to what it had been in its glamour days, perhaps. She'd wandered through the grounds, passing the locked cottage, used once again for school visits, and into a part of the grounds she hadn't visited before. The sunken Tuscan garden, filled with graceful statues and a stone bench. It had felt familiar, and she'd sat on the bench and known that this place was Belle's, that this safe, warm place had been her ward. Amelia had felt Belle's spirit and known she was close, that she was happy in her forest, not scared and hunted but free. A child.

To do that, to make things as right as they could be, had been like a balm to Amelia. To be able to tell Robert his sister was at rest, to let Jean know her actions had turned out right, had felt great. She wanted to do that for others.

"No. I think it's great." He smirked. "Want an assistant? I do a great line in knowing when to run." His face sobered. "And – I don't want you where I can't hold you."

She joined him on the bed, tracing his stomach muscles with her finger, running it over his skin, so that he shivered.

"Do you know?" she said. "I just might."

THE END

Dear Reader

Thank you for reading *The Wildest Hunt*. If you enjoyed this book (or even if you didn't) please consider leaving a star rating or review online. Your feedback is important, and will help other readers to find the book and decide whether to read it, too.

Acknowledgements

I had a blast writing The Wildest Hunt. It came to me on a holiday, on a lovely summer's day at Glenveagh in Donegal, and ended up as a snowy, wintery story. The journey to write a book is another that takes longer than it seems it will!

Firstly to the beta readers! Three early readers who, as ever, have to wade through the roughest versions and seek any diamonds that might be hidden. Kerry, Dom and Panu – thank you so much! And then the community who take the questions, read excerpts, give moral support – I have many of these but a special call out needs to go to the writing community at SFFChronicles and to the Northern Irish community at OtherworldsNI. Really, if you're a writer, go find your tribe. They do the best cake.

And then to the publishers. Inspired Quill, who have a lovely community of writers, ably supported by Sara-Jayne Slack. They're always a pleasure to work with, thoughtful editors, and great cheerleaders who deserve, as always, a thank you for taking a chance on this little book.

Of course, the family and friends who turn up at events, who cheerlead and support, and who put up with distracted me.

And, lastly, the readers, who support and encourage and who, I hope, will like this little one. ☺ In the meantime, don't get too comfy. It's winter, in Donegal, it's cold and it's dark. And so the Hunt begins.

Jo x

About the Author

Jo writes mostly-dark sci-fi and fantasy, sometimes in her native Northern Ireland, sometimes in her space opera world. She's been writing for almost a decade and is the author of The Inheritance Trilogy and Inish Carraig, both sci-fi books, as well as Waters and the Wild, a dark fairy tale set in the beguiling Glens of Antrim.

When she's not writing, Jo also runs The Secret Bookshelf, a bookshop in Carrickfergus, with her husband, Chris.

Find the author via her website: www.jozebedee.com

Or tweet at her: @jozebwrites

More From This Author

Waters And The Wild

Amy's heard the voices all her life.

The doctors insist they're in her mind. Her mother believes they are fae. Amy knows they have turned deadly.

While attending a wedding deep in the Antrim glens, the voices grow darker and their song takes hold. Not sure if she's mad or if her mother is correct, she flees, drawing well-meaning Simon into her terrifying road trip.

Now Amy knows she must defeat the voices once and for all. To escape their hold, she must confront long-hidden secrets, and find a truth which may not be hers to unearth.

But, even then, the fairies may not let her go…

Inish Carraig

The invasion is over. Humanity has lost.

In Belfast, John Dray protects his younger siblings by working for the local hard man. Set up, he gets sent to the formidable alien prison, Inish Carraig, a fate Henry Carter, the policeman assigned to John, can't stop.

Once there, John discovers a plot which threatens Earth and everyone he loves. To reveal it, he has to get out of the prison – and there is only one person who can help. The stakes are raised for both men – and humanity needs them to act.

A bestseller about Alien Invasion, Inish Carraig is 'blessed with an entirely novel storyline' (Alexander Stevenson-Kaatsch).

Available from all major online and offline outlets.